CHARLIE'S ANGELS II:

A Polyamorous Affair

PENNY BLACWRITE

For Shyann ...
The first girl I ever loved.

PENNY BLACWRITE'S CATALOG

NOTE TO READER

Whoa! Whoa! Whoa! Back up, baby. Before you read this book,

you must download

<u>BOOK ONE</u> *Charlie's Angels: A Polyamorous Affair!*

Make sure you read, rate, & review!

Trigger Warning

This book contains domestic violence, drugs, taboo sex practices, and LGBTQ sex. Also, there is a glossary at the end of the book full of New York lingo and other cultural sayings present in the book for your convenience and enjoyment. Please check it out.

1
LIPSTICK LESBIAN
SHENELLE "SHELLY" FOX

*"*W*HAT THE FUCK WAS THAT ABOUT?" I ASKED* Sean, nearly badgering him after Charlie franticly stormed out of the penthouse.

With arms folded and nostrils flaring, Sean's face was stone cold, and his chin chiseled and stiff. "Do you really want to be a stepmother to my first child with a stranger?"

"Stepmother? Desean, we will be involved whether or not that baby is yours. Charlie is a part of this family now!"

Sean shook his head several times. "You just refuse to give up this lesbian shit, huh? Do you see what your perverted lust has got us into? How the fuck do you think it makes me feel to have my first child with a woman I barely even know rather than my wife?"

Sean's words hit me in the heart like a dagger. He thought I was some sick lesbo with a weird obsession because I loved women. He couldn't understand why I wasn't totally fulfilled just being a rich man's wife. While I loved Sean and was in love with him, his love just wasn't enough for me. All the while, I thought he understood my needs. I thought we were on the same page, but he threw my lesbianism in my face whenever he felt like it. I was boiling with anger at hearing him bring up his desire for children when he knew getting pregnant was always a struggle for us.

With shaky hands, I stepped forward, looking deeply into his eyes. "Listen, you know how much I would love to give you children, but you know what we're up against," I tried to reason before I got super emotional.

"No, Shenelle! I don't know what we're up against because you've never talked about it candidly with me." Sean's eyes were straining as a vein in his temple protruded forward. "You haven't allowed me in your doctor's visits, and out of respect for you and your medical privacy, I never pushed it. Still, I am your husband, and I'm tired of dancing around this shit."

I raised my hand to his chest, hoping my touch would calm him down, for I was afraid of what he would say next. Sean knew my tactics and slapped my hand off of him. "Stop trying to control everything, stop trying to manipulate me, and let me get this out," he scoffed.

I stepped back, offended, and watched his every move.

"We're both pushing forty. We're wealthy with no children and nobody to pass down our wealth or legacy to, and instead of focusing our efforts on getting you whatever you need so we can conceive and build our family, you want to chase women and have a fuck fest!"

Tears welled up in my eyes, and a knot invaded my chest. I felt like

I couldn't breathe. Sean had never spoken to me this way. *We've never spoken to each other this way.* Wiping my face with the back of my hand, I looked at his soft, distressed eyes. "It's just not that simple."

Sean invaded my space and grabbed my hands into his. "Baby, we have enough money and resources to make it easier than the average person. Despite how much I don't want to be with other women, I do it to please you. Can't you try to give me what I want for once? Please understand there's nothing more I want in this world than a baby with the love of my life, my wife." His eyes were watery now too, and I could feel him submitting as he pleaded with me. However, I just couldn't receive it or get past the hurt.

With tears falling and staining my face, I held my chin up, facing him with an austere expression. "You could forget about that ever happening because your wife's ovaries are dead." I backed away from him slowly, watching his cheeks seep into his face and a lone tear fall. "Don't bother me today. I'll be back later," I declared before turning away and heading into the silo bathroom.

As I sat on the toilet, whimpering, I grabbed my phone off the sink and did something I knew I had to do. I scrolled down my phonebook, clicked on Shyann's name, and started composing a text.

Me: *I need to see you. Meet me at Brooklyn Museum for First Fridays at 3 p.m.*

In a matter of one minute, she texted me back with a smiley face emoji.

Shyann: *Long time no hear. I'll be there. I can't wait to see you.*

Me: *Neither can I!!!*

Shyann: *I hope there's not trouble in paradise. You know how much I hate coming between you and Sean.*

Me: *I miss the old Shyann, who didn't give a fuck about my husband.*

Shyann: *I'm getting older. I'm looking to settle down, not play cat-and-mouse, Shenelle.*

I twiddled my thumbs as I studied her text. Shyann has never been one to play coy with me, and as much as I knew that meeting up with her would be testy, I knew I needed to do it. I needed to see her face. I needed to vent. I needed her wisdom. I needed her to touch my hand, caress it gently, and tell me I was strong and could have whatever I wanted, just as she did when I met her as a nineteen-year-old pursuing AKA. I needed that nurturing from a prophyte, a woman I admired, and a woman I once deeply loved. More importantly, I needed a friend, someone who knew me on deeper levels than my husband.

Me*: I know. I know. I'm not here to lead you on or play with you. I just need a friend to talk to.*

Shyann: *Understood. See you this afternoon, Shenelle.*

From the dismissiveness of her last text, I knew Shyann was hurting. She remained single all these years, hoping that one day, I'd leave Sean and live happily ever after with her. As much as I thought about it frequently, I could never disrespect my marital vows. If Shyann couldn't get with the program of polyamory, we'd be nothing more than friends.

2

SISTERLY LOVE

CHARLESTINA "CHARLIE" THOMPSON

I *STOOD IN FRONT OF SADE'S APARTMENT, SHIVERING* with fear of judgment. How in the hell was I supposed to tell my best friend that I was pregnant and didn't know if the father was Rodney or Sean? As much as I didn't want to tell her, as much as I just wanted to disappear and roll up into a ball and cry, I knew I needed emotional support. I took a deep breath, inhaling the stale smell of NYCHA (New York City Housing Authority), better known as the projects, and knocked on Sade's door. A few minutes later, after looking through the peephole, she opened the heavy brass door and let me in.

"Charlie, what's wrong?" she asked as she pulled me into her dimly lit hallway. As soon as I saw her, tears welled up in my eyes. I was shivering and shaking.

"What happened, babe? Was it Rodney? Did he hurt you?" She walked me into her living room and sat me on her couch. Two of her sons were sitting in front of the TV.

"Go downstairs to Ms. B's house. I'll text you when you can come back," she instructed them.

They huffed and puffed and got up from their seats. With their heads down, they walked past us, groaning.

"Fix y'all face. It won't be long," Sade assured them.

Her oldest son, Joshua, turned around and said, "Whatever you're going through, Ms. Charlie, I hope you feel better." His kind words warmed my heart, reminding me of Jaden.

Jaden was so sweet as a young boy before he got dragged into the gang life. Although I loved the opportunities that came with moving to New York, I hated my son felt so lost and lonely that he became a Crip member, but I was happy that I was able to steer him away from the gang life and that now he was doing well.

"Thank you, Joshua!"

"No problem," he replied, following behind his brother out the door.

"Your boys are so sweet," I complimented Sade.

"I appreciate it, babe, but what's going on?"

I gritted my teeth and pursed my lips. "Sade, I'm pregnant."

Sade's eyes lit up as she covered her mouth. "What? OMG baby, congrats!"

Her insensitivity and obliviousness caused me to cry a bit more. This should have been a joyous time, yet I was full of confusion.

Resting her hand on my shoulder, she said, "Don't cry, baby. Don't cry."

I wiped my eyes and quickly got myself together, exhaling several breaths.

"How is Shelly taking it, knowing you're pregnant by her husband?" Sade eagerly asked.

"Shelly seems happy. It's Sean who's not, and frankly, neither am I," I admitted.

An overlay of confusion showed up on Sade's face. She was really starting to annoy the fuck out of me, acting like I should be so fucking happy to be pregnant without a husband or man to call my own.

"How come, babe?"

"Are you fucking serious right now, Sade? I'm thirty-four, never married, with a twenty-one-year-old son. Why the fuck would I want to bring another child into this world out of wedlock? I'm basically a side chick. The only difference is that the wife knows about me," I chided.

Sade placed her hand on my thigh, and her confused face turned into a sympathetic ploy. "I'm sorry, babe," was all she could say.

"And the worst thing about this all is the fact that until this baby comes, there's no telling if it's Sean's baby or Rodney's."

Sade's doe eyes bulged as she pinched her lips between her thumb and index finger. "Fuck, girl. Damn. So, you're really thinking about keeping it?"

"Of course! That's without a doubt. I was raised in the South girl. We don't believe in abortions. My granny would roll over in her grave if I went and had a fucking abortion."

Sade scrunched her face and sucked her teeth. "Girl bye. It's not that fucking serious. If you don't want the baby, have a fucking abortion. Point blank, period."

Sade could be so insensitive at times. That was one thing I hated about her. Not knowing what would come out of her mouth was also another thing I hated.

"That's not even up for debate, so drop it, Sade," I asserted.

Rolling her eyes, huffing and puffing, she said, "Well, what are you going to do?"

I gulped and swallowed hard before rubbing my chin. "I'm gon' take care of my baby."

Sade chuckled and shook her head. "Now, if this baby is Sean's, you'll be set for life, but if this baby is Rodney, you'll be on your own, babe. Do you really think you could endure that again, especially after Jaden's practically out of the house and a grown-ass man?"

I pondered on her statement. I hadn't raised an infant in over fifteen years. *Was I really going to start all over again?*

"I guess I'll have to because an abortion is out of the question. Jaden is about to graduate summa cum laude with a job in the tech field, making seventy thousand dollars a year. By the time he's thirty, he'll be making two hundred thousand dollars or more. I could have aborted him, but if I had, we wouldn't have the next Black Bill Gates."

"You know I hate it when you bring that up because it makes me so angry. You had no business having a child that young. Abortion is necessary in some cases."

I jumped up off her sofa and folded my arms. "It wasn't necessary for me, and that's why I didn't do it. A child is a blessing. Who am I to steal the blessing God gave me from the world?"

"Charlie, you were a child yourself when you had Jaden!" she protested.

"Well, I'm grown now, and I'm keeping this baby!" I defended myself.

"Are you going to tell Rodney?"

I stopped myself before speaking because I didn't want to say too much that would let it away that Rodney had raped me. Encouraging me to abort my baby was one thing, but I couldn't handle her making light of my sexual assault. I couldn't stand for that.

"Nope. I figured I'd just worked it out with Sean and Shelly. Once the baby gets here, we will test Sean for paternity. If he's the father, there's no need to reach out to Rodney. If Sean isn't the father, I'll cross that bridge when I get there!" I declared.

Sade twisted her lip and shrugged her shoulders. "Ehh. If you like it, I love it. Either way, I'm here to support you, and you better make me the godmother!" Sade said in a playful manner as she stood up and wrapped her arms around me. "One thing I know for sure is that baby will be loved because you're a great mother to Jaden, and you'll be an even greater mother now. I know I can be harsh at times, but I just want the best for you."

I hugged her back and rested my head on her shoulder.

"I know, girl. Just work on your delivery because there are a lot of things that I butter up before telling you just to make sure that you receive the message."

Rubbing my head with her hand, she giggled. "I know, I know, Ms.

Southern Belle. I'll work on it!"

"Good! Now call them kids back upstairs and get ready. I'm taking y'all out for dinner!"

Sade let me go and jumped up explosively with her arms pried open. "Yes, girl! Where are we going?"

"Wherever you want!"

"You're far too kind. I should be the one taking you out."

I grabbed her by the hand and shook my head. "No, you shouldn't. Just having you as a friend, despite how irritating your ass is, is good enough for me. Besides, I need to be around some love. Can I sleep over?" I asked.

"Of course, you can, babe."

"Thanks, boo. You know you're the only family I got outside of Jaden," I admitted aloud, even to myself for the first time.

"And you're the only family I've got outside of my boys, but as long as we got each other, we'll be all right," Sade said and hugged me again.

Having a friend who would support and uplift you when your dead weight was overwhelming and even burdensome proved loyalty and true love. I was grateful to have a friend like Sade, even though she wasn't perfect, because truthfully, who the fuck really was?

3

BEST THING I NEVER HAD

DESEAN "SEAN" FOX

"I *WAS SHOCKED WHEN I GOT A TEXT MESSAGE FROM* you. It's been how long? A year? Two years?" Gina, who was even more attractive than I last remembered questioned.

Sitting across from her in her quaint modern-like office situated in Dumbo, I studied her from the waist up. Her perky breasts sat beautifully in her plunge blouse below her long eyelashes, rosy plump lips, and blemish-free dark chocolate skin, not to mention she had the best set of shiny white teeth I'd seen. I bit my bottom lip as I checked her out. Gina was a knockout. Although it was visible that she had gained a bit of weight, she was wearing it well. In fact, she looked better than ever before.

"Maybe three years. It has been a while, though," I confirmed as I studied Gina's bright smile and sculpted calves as she crossed her legs.

Gina was wearing peep-toe pumps, and her toes were painted a rose pink that illuminated beautifully on her skin.

"Indeed. What brings you in today? Is there something, in particular, bothering you?"

I exhaled deeply. My breath was raspy, and the smell of mint hit my nostrils. I made sure that I ate a peppermint on my way driving here.

"I'm having issues in my marriage, and I need to talk about them with someone that knows my wife and me."

Gina scrunched her brows. "You, of all people, know I specialize in trauma and grief-related counseling. I don't do well with family issues."

"I know, Gina, but I need you," I sternly stated as I leaned forward in my chair.

Gina's eyes softened, and her shoulders relaxed as a calm smile spread across her face. "Okay, if you insist, Sean. What's going on with you and Shelly?"

Interlocking my fingers and cracking my knuckles, I pondered on what I would say first. I exhaled from my nose and just spoke the truth.

"Shelly and I added a woman to our relationship," I confessed.

Gina's eyes squinched as she studied me. "Interesting. Go on."

"Don't look at me like that." I chuckled to lighten the mood. "It was all Shelly's idea, and this isn't our first time doing this. Throughout the years, Shelly has always insisted that women join us in the bedroom. It started from just casual threesomes and progressed to full-blown relationships."

"Well, do you enjoy these arrangements?"

"No. I hate them. I hate sharing my wife. I hate allowing other women into our bedroom. I hate seeing the joy and pleasure on my wife's face when she looks at a woman, especially when she's having sex with another woman. It's like she's in paradise. It bothers me that I'm not enough for her." Admitting those feelings aloud made them real, not only for me but for Gina.

"Ahh, I understand. Your feelings are valid. So, tell me, have you expressed your concerns to Shelly? Have you told her how sharing her makes you feel?"

"Not exactly, because the last thing I want to do is articulate my weakness for her. I already display it by participating in it. To beg her to stop would make me feel more emasculated than now."

Gina nodded her head. "Hmm. I guess I can understand that."

I looked behind Gina and settled on a crystallized art piece that sat on her olive-colored walls. The earthy tone of her office was also accompanied by a clean, fresh linen fragrance that kept me alert and able to compose myself despite the emotions I was battling.

"Nonetheless, this situation with Charlie, the newest girl, poses a real threat to our relationship."

"How so?"

"We just found out that she's pregnant."

Gina gasped and bit her bottom lip. "Wow. I have so many questions. Are you guys certain it's your baby? Not that you can ever be certain until a paternity test is involved, but you know what I mean. Was she seeing anyone else?"

"Yes, and no. Charlie had just ended her last relationship with her ex, some abusive loser-type nigga. She got away from him and moved in with us, only for him to stalk and rape her. So truthfully, it's no telling if

I'm the baby's father or if her ex is."

"Ahh, I see. That's both equally dramatic and traumatic. Yikes." Gina sighed. "Well, how is Shelly taking the news?"

"Surprisingly, she's ecstatic."

"And I take it you aren't."

I clenched my jaw and folded my arms across my chest. "Why the fuck would I be? Why would I want to have my first child with a stranger?" I angrily bucked.

"And why wouldn't Shelly, of all people, understand that?" she added, filling in the gap.

"Exactly, and more importantly, why wouldn't Shelly want to give me a child?" I croaked with a shaky voice.

"Does she just not want children? Is it because of both of your demanding careers? What do you think it is?"

I scratched my chin. "I don't know exactly, but Shelly has never been pregnant by me. She doesn't even get her menstrual regularly. In the beginning of our marriage, it wasn't much of an issue because we were both career-focused beasts, especially her since she was determined to never experience poverty or living paycheck to paycheck ever again."

Gina sat up in her chair, raising her head as if she had an epiphany. "Right, unlike you who came into your father's estate in your early twenties, Shelly wasn't afforded that. She was groomed to work hard for everything."

"Exactly, and it doesn't matter that I'm the first and only Black CEO of New York's most prestigious hospital. Shelly refuses to play into the traditional wife role."

"And you're just willing to accept this, Sean? You both aren't getting any younger. Shelly's losing eggs every day. Fortunately for you, you can remarry and still have children until the day you die. Are you really going to settle for being in a marriage where you can't continue your legacy?" Gina was intently staring at me as she waited on me to answer.

I shook my head back and forth and shrugged. "I don't know. I guess so. I'm still deeply in love with Shelly."

"But why? She doesn't respect you. She's not satisfied with you, and clearly, she isn't deeply in love with you. Come on, we both know Shelly is a bonafide lesbian." Gina didn't hold back her disdain as she spoke.

"Watch your mouth when talking about my wife," I warned Gina as I spat with venom through seething teeth. *How fucking dare she?*

Gina twisted her lip as she raised out of her chair. She placed her hands on her hips, exaggerating her stance.

"You texted me, paid me double my rate to clear my calendar just to see you, knowing that not only do I not specialize in family issues, but more importantly, that I'm not fond of Shelly at all. You come in here complaining to me about your marriage, a woman who would never treat you the way she does. A woman who was madly in love with you and has not been able to move on and find love yet. Do you think this shit is easy for me to bear?" Gina swallowed some tears as she heaved.

I knew what we had was special, but I honestly thought that she got over it and moved on. Gina was a catch. Any man would be happy to have her.

I stood up and rushed to her side. "I'm sorry, Gina. I had no idea."

She pushed me away and disagreed, "Yes, you did! You broke off a good thing, a sweet thing that we had to run back to Shelly as soon as she broke it off with Shyann."

"Gina, you and I couldn't continue our relationship once I found out you two were line sisters. Even if I never got back with Shelly, I couldn't have taken you seriously."

With damp eyes, Gina cocked her head to the side. "Meanwhile, she can fuck our prophyte on and off for years, but you couldn't see past the letters that you and I were perfect for each other?"

I felt Gina's pain. I really did, but I couldn't empathize with her.

"Gina, you're a great woman. You're beautiful and dynamic, but what we had wasn't magical. We weren't perfect for each other because every day I spent with you, I couldn't get Shelly out of my mind, which is why I married her."

Gina's pursed lips and flat gaze said it all. Tears streamed down the side of her cheek as she walked away from me, toward the door. "It doesn't matter what you do, nothing will ever please Shelly. She adds woman after woman to your relationship, hoping to replace Shyann, the real love of her life. Hopefully, you recognize this before she humiliates you more than you could ever hurt me!" Gina's face tightened. "Have a good evening, Desean, and don't you ever in your fucking life call me again!"

Gina opened the door and grilled me up and down as I glided past her. As I walked to the elevator, my heart jumped. Gina was absolutely right about Shelly. I could no longer lie to myself.

4
JUST A FRIEND
SHELLY

BROOKLYN MUSEUM BECAME EVEN MORE ECLECTIC in the last few years than ever before. With the growing influx of transplants and gentrification as the new norm, everything about Brooklyn Museum was artsy and quirky. From the abstract décor, the stragglers that paced up and down and all around the corners bordering Grand Army Plaza, and the teenagers loitering outside, Brooklyn Museum was home to many. I remember coming here for the first time with Shyann at least fifteen years ago, and here I was again. Yet this time, I was chasing her, instead of the other way around.

Spotting her from behind as she stood in front of the avant-garde-dressed mannequins that filled up the Mugler's exhibit, I quietly glided near her. I wore a pair of flats today so my words would be felt rather than heard and so that I was in close proximity to her.

Leaning down, I whispered into her ear, catching her completely off guard, "Good afternoon, darling."

She turned around in a panic, with a combination of commotion and confusion written all over her face. "Oh, fuck Shelly! Don't do that! You scared the fuck out of me," Shyann complained.

"Boo!" I playfully etched, my voice mimicking a creepy monster in a horror movie.

"Still Silly Shelly. I guess some things never change!" Shyann, laughed, revealing her sexy mouth and quirky lisp that drove me crazy.

She was right, and the same applied to her. From the physical, not much had changed. She was still sporting her bold afro, that was bigger than ever. She was still rocking androgynous looks while dressed in a patchwork patterned two-piece pantsuit. She topped it off with some soft feminine accents like her signature French tip full set that complimented her dainty hands so well and a red lipstick that sat on the curve of her upper lip, just calling and enticing me to smear the makeup off her pretty face. One distinct thing I noticed was that Shyann looked several years younger. Her deep chocolate skin was blemish free, radiant, and bright, and she looked like she'd dropped a few pounds.

"Some things never do, yet somehow they're never the same," I noted as I leaned in for a kiss. Instead of pecking Shyann on the lips, she turned her face, causing me to catch her cheek. Our eyes met after the exchange, and I could feel the apprehension in the air.

"Hmm. If it was up to you, I know you'd love for everything to change while you still remain the same," Shyann displeasingly stated as she shrugged her shoulders.

I chuckled and rolled my eyes. "Can we at least have lunch before we argue? A bitch is hungry!" I joked, desperate to lighten the mood.

"Sure, after you enjoy the Mugler exhibit with me. I'm so impressed by it.”

“You should be. Your hard work has certainly paid off. Do you remember when you told me years ago that you would be the first Black queer museum curator in New York? Look at you now. You're not only the first but also the best and most distinguished of this millennium.”

Shyann blushed at my compliment as she started to walk around the perimeter of the mannequins.

I shuffled toward her and grabbed her by the arm. “I'm proud of you, Shy Shy,” I expressed as I picked up her hand and kissed it.

The softness of her skin against my lips felt like velvet and smelled divine. A tingle belted from my stomach down the pubs of my landing strip, and that's when I knew I was still in love with Shyann. I honestly thought that after the last blow out Sean, Shy, and I had, I could never feel this way about her, but that never changed.

Shyann allowed me to kiss her hand before caressing mine. The electric spark between us shot signals to my brain. Shyann was the only person who made me feel this way, yet I couldn't have her.

“Thank you. What do you have a taste for? There's Caribbean, Italian, Indian, and All-American if you want to take a walk. If not, we can grab a bite from the museum food mart.”

The sound of a stroll excited me. “Let's take a walk, just like old times.”

Shyann squinched her eyes, shifting her gaze to the side, and produced a sly, mysterious look.

“All right then, let's go.”

We made our way out of the museum and walked up Eastern Parkway. The weather was as uncomfortable as we both were. Between concealing the truth with warm, fuzzy pleasantries, the cold air still loomed over us. We walked at least a mile without saying a word, just enjoying the sound of the thuds from our boots slamming against the pavement.

Just as I became comfortable with the awkward silence and the wisp from the slowly budding trees, Shyann yanked me back from crossing the street.

"Look, Shelly. I can't do this tiptoeing bullshit with you. If you have something you want to say to me, I suggest you do it before we get into a closed area. I'd rather hash it out here and let the birds hear us than get into a heated argument in one of my favorite establishments I frequent on the regular."

I should have known her cool demeanor was too good to be true. If anyone knew how serious and exact Shyann was, it was me. She was not one for games, which always had me questioning why she had put up with my bullshit all these years.

Struggling to find the words to say, I just blurted out the first thing on the tip of my tongue. "Sean and I are having a baby."

Shyann's eyes sparked up but only for a second until her face caved in, followed by a flat, dull gaze. "You're pregnant, Shelly?"

"No," I answered quickly.

Her eyes widened and her pupils enlarged as I witnessed rage crawl under her skin. "Sean's cheating?" she asked as her brow raised.

"No. Our girlfriend, Charlie, is pregnant."

"What! You can't be fucking forreal, Shenelle."

"As cancer," I answered.

Shyann stormed off, scurrying across the street as she swiftly avoided traffic. I waited for two cars to roll by before I rushed after her.

"What the fuck, Shyann? I came to you because you were the only person who I could trust with this kind of information. I need you right now."

Tension rose in her shoulders as sharp as her chin locked. "Really, Shenelle? What the fuck can I do for you this time? What advice do you want from me?"

I shrugged while defeat depleted me. Shyann rarely got angry. Even after breaking her heart several times before, she never raised her voice at me. Stepping forward, I grabbed her by the face and kissed her passionately before trickling my hand down and fondling her breasts from outside of her shirt. Her lips were as soft and moist as red velvet cake. I held onto her lips, savoring the kiss, before letting her go.

"I just want you to listen and comfort me. Tell me everything is going to be okay. Tell me it's okay if Sean's first child isn't by me because I'll eventually be able to carry his baby," I simpered, wiping away tears.

Tightening her mouth with a plastered-on screw face, Shyann shook her head slowly. "No, Shenelle! I can't tell you that because it's not true. You've had over five abortions and several miscarriages. Children just might not be in the future for you," she threateningly sneered as if she loathed me.

Her words ached as painfully as my first miscarriage, feeling like blood was leaking out of me from how carelessly she spoke.

"And no, you can't come waltzing into my life, playing with my heart, kissing me, and thinking that changes anything. You chose Sean and now you have to live with it."

I swallowed Shyann's condemnation, staring directly into her despairing face, trying my best to block out the busyness behind her, from the school kids bustling down the street and honking horns. Although I was fighting a visual distraction, my heart was still in pieces, and no amount of commotion could put me at ease.

"But Shyann, you always know what to say. You've always been my rock, and I know you felt the underlying passion of that kiss," I pleaded.

Pointing an accusatory finger at me, Shyann jumped back. "No! No, I didn't, Shelly. I am not your garbage can. I am not here for you to just dump and dump and pile your emotional baggage on me. Do you realize I haven't heard from you in two years? Not a check-in call or text during the pandemic. My mother died, and you didn't even pick up the phone. All you did was like a post on Facebook!" Shyann was irate as angry tears fell from her face. The baritone of her voice deepened, yet her words were as clear as day. "Yet here I go, trying to be captain save a hoe. As soon as you called, I came running, thinking you would change. Thinking that the next time I heard from you, you'd come back to me for good, recognizing that I'm the love of your life, but it's evident that you'll choose anybody over me," Shyann cried, allowing the tears to stain her face.

I reached out to grab her, and she smacked my hand out of the way.

"Don't touch me!"

Not fazed, I reached forward again, and she shoved me away even harder.

"Just stop. Stop it, Shenelle. Don't say a fucking word. I don't want to hear your crafty pivot or the bullshit flavorful language you conjure out of your ass. I just want you to vanish and never call me again," she stammered before trudging away. Her short legs peddled down the block in record time, one of the briskest walks I've ever seen.

Shyann left me freezing and naked in the cold with an empty vessel as a heart and a perplexed and contorted mind. It didn't matter how long I stayed away from Shyann. I never suspected that she would be the one to leave me indefinitely.

By the time I got back home, my mind was so cloudy that I barely even noticed Sean as I stumbled back in. He was sitting cross-legged on the sofa, reading a journal, an iPad to his right, and a laptop to his left. Sean's eyes beamed once he saw me. Despair had to be written all over my face because his brows raised as soon as he made eye contact with me.

"Baby, what's wrong?" he asked, his tone riddled with concern.

I couldn't even look at him or process his words. My shoulders drooped and my head low. I shuffled past him. The truth was that Sean would always be here, but I had just lost the true love of my life.

Walking forward through the house, I heard the muffles of Sean's words. "Baby, talk to me."

Finally, in the room, I slammed the door behind me, drowning out his continuous echo. I just needed to be alone. There was nothing he could do or say to un-break my heart. Shyann had torn it out and shredded it into pieces.

5
WHOLESOME
CHARLIE

Sade did her best to make me feel as comfortable as possible in her three-bedroom project apartment. While I had never spent more than one night in the projects, these last few days assured me it wasn't that bad. From how nicely Sade had decked out her apartment, you would have never known we were in the projects. From her plush, expensive furniture, including a freestanding cream-colored bar adorned with endless bottles of Moet, and an antique sofa set, Sade was living large. I had never seen such elaborate furniture until I came to her place.

Growing up in Lagrange, Georgia, family and neighbors had decent-sized homes, but the décor of their houses was old-fashioned and country. Despite having not even a quarter of the space I grew up with down south, Sade decorated her quaint castle with all the bells and whistles. Most importantly, her home was full of love.

This was my fourth day waking up at Sade's house to the smells of homemade breakfast and soft music. Cinnamon and Erykah Badu went together well. Stepping out of the full-sized bed, I stretched, elongating my limbs, and sighed. I stepped into the slippers that Sade gave me and bowed to the life-size cut-out of Kobe Bryant plastered on the wall.

"Good morning Kobe," I greeted the image and smiled.

After Sade's son Joshua so graciously allowed me to sleep in his room, he said the least I could do was acknowledge Kobe every morning. Joshua was fifteen years old and sweet. Although it was clear that he was a regular around-the-way boy with dreams of making it to the NBA, he was well-mannered and respectful.

I picked up my phone from the nightstand, and it immediately vibrated. Shelly's name flashed across the screen. As I looked at her name blare on the screen again and again, I shook my head and ignored the call. I just wasn't in the mood. I needed some space to figure out what the fuck I was going to do about this pregnancy. Although, I boasted about having the baby to Sade the other day, truthfully, I was conflicted. Considering how early I was, I had the option of having an abortion, which I had been contemplating the last few days. Yet, seeing how much Sade's youngest son hugged her and gave her kisses melted my heart. Being here the last few days was giving me baby fever.

I'd happily keep the baby if I knew without a shadow of a doubt that Sean was my child's father. However, knowing that there was a possibility that Rodney had impregnated me had my mind full of doubt. For the last few days, I woke up, repeatedly replaying the same scenario in my head, thinking of how I would explain myself to Jaden and how I'd have to come clean to Sade about Rodney raping me if he were really the father.

Arrgh.

Today, I was determined to have a good day and push those disturbing thoughts into the back of my mind. I needed just one day to enjoy being carefree. Why not start it with a savory breakfast? As I opened the door, a rush of nutmeg and burnt butter hit me, filling my senses with memories of my momma's country cooking. Walking through the apartment toward the kitchen, I felt a ray of sunshine dance over me. The one thing I did like about Sade's apartment was how much sunlight passed through, bouncing off the walls and painting a bright shadow over the furniture. Despite how foul-smelling the lobby was and how much garbage sat in front of the building, there was a calmness, stillness, and love throughout Sade's apartment. There was an unconditional, sweet kind of love that permeated through the walls of her apartment that didn't exist in my loft that I shared with Rodney or even the plush penthouse that I now shared with the Fox's.

"Good morning!" Sade greeted me, fully dressed in jeans and a sweater. I peered down at my phone. And it was only seven o'clock in the morning.

"Morning!" I yawned, stretching my arms, and rolling my shoulders back. "You're up early and fully dressed again. It's Saturday, Sade! Do you not ever just sleep in or sport loungewear?"

Sade shook her head frivolously. "Girl, no. I'm a boy mom. My sons have never seen me in my underwear, let alone naked."

I scrunched my nose and twisted my lip. "You can't be serious!" I stammered.

"Very serious! Boys are very visual, and besides, I want them to choose a good girl, so I have to show them a good representation of women. Now is prime time, especially since they are teenagers."

"I guess you're right," I agreed. "Well, where are the boys, anyway?"

"At the store," Sade stated as she walked toward the fridge and opened it. Her kitchen and dining area were so small and quaint but decorated with wholesome love. From the knickknacks on the wall, the accents she held her dish washing liquid in, and the magnets on her refrigerator door, nostalgia hit me, reminding me of what an actual home felt like. Sade may have lived in the projects, but the feel of her 1050-square-foot apartment was nothing short of the Huxtables.

"My boys may be sheltered, but I'm raising them as men. They know how to grocery shop, cook, and budget money. I can't afford to enable my black boys. Their grandmother did that, which explains why their father ain't shit." Sade winced.

I cracked a smile and forced a laugh despite how painful her words actually were. Raising black boys as a single mother isn't easy. I knew all about it, and sadly Sade's words were valid. Loving on black boys too much and not preparing them to handle responsibility enabled them and set the next generation up to fail. As black mothers, we'd be doing the entire community a disservice.

"Anyway, I've got pancakes and French toast. Which would you like?" Sade asked.

Just before I got to answer, my loud ringtone interrupted my thoughts. I pulled out the phone, expecting to see Shelly's number. Instead, it was

Sean.

"Shelly again?" Sade inquired.

Hesitantly, I shook my head as Sade's cheeks puffed out while she stared at me. Raising her shoulders, she asked, "Who is it?"

"It's Sean," I muttered.

Sade's eyes bulged so wide you would have thought she saw Casper. "Answer it! This is the first time he's calling, right?"

"Yes!" I exclaimed as I held the ringing phone in my hand, looking down at Sean's name bounce across the screen.

Shaking, I answered, "Hello."

Somehow I could hear uneasiness in Sean's methodical breathing, which made me antsier than needed.

"Charlie, are you okay?" Sean asked in a concerned tone.

I rolled my eyes so hard they almost got lost in the back of my head. Sade stood a few feet from me, holding her hand over her mouth and laughing.

"Yes, Sean, I'm fine. How can I help you?"

"Charlie, I'm sorry for being so cold and kicking you out. It was a lot for me to process."

With my hand on my hip, I spoke into the phone slowly. "Uh-huh."

"For real, Charlie. Look, we need to talk. Can you meet me at Red Rooster in Harlem in two hours?"

"No!" I asserted abruptly, allowing a few seconds to go by. The other end of the phone was quiet long enough, so I knew Sean was rattled. "I'm in Brooklyn," I added.

Sean exhaled slowly and said, "No problem. I'll come to you. Can you meet me at Shane's on Washington Avenue? They have the best brunch in Brooklyn."

"No!" I reiterated. "But you can come to get me, and we can go there together. I'll text you my address. I'll be ready by noon. See you soon, Sean," I stated and immediately hung up.

"Damn girl, you're cold," Sade butted in.

"Ice cold, baby. Ice cold."

I made Sean sit in quiet agony the entire car ride, reserving all my conversation for the table at Shane's. Now sitting across from him swirling my tongue around the straw, I stared into his eyes, searching for his heart. His usual cold grimace had faded, and his sympathetic eyes presented a blush of compassion, which threw me by surprise. Dressed more casually than I had ever seen, Sean raised the fitted hat off his head and placed it on the table before resting his hand on top of mine. Despite the spring weather blooming, his hand was cold.

Gazing around the nearly empty restaurant that smelled savory with a sting of depletion, I took in my surroundings. Not that I was hiding from anyone or anything. I just exhibited the natural tendency of always being alert, a side effect of living in New York.

"Charlie, thanks for agreeing to meet with me," Sean finally said.

I tightened my lip, preparing the words to roll out but to no effect. Instead, I nodded my head, this time not deliberately giving him the silent treatment. In fact, I was so fixated on cutting my chicken and red velvet waffles into quartered pieces.

"The way I reacted to the discovery of your pregnancy was wrong and cold," he expressed flatly, almost aloof, yet somehow I knew that was his way of being sincere.

"Yes, it was," I asserted, dropping my knife and fork into a pool of syrup.

"I know I was the least bit of compassionate, but it was a lot to take in," Sean exasperated. "Truth be told, I'm a one woman's man. I've never been into the threesomes or anything poly. In the past, I'd only participated to please Shelly, but never in a million years did I think that I'd be having my first child with a woman my wife and I brought into our bedroom. How the hell are we supposed to tell our child that they were the product of a sex-crazed poly relationship? Outside of that, how am I supposed to introduce my child to the world without them getting all into my and Shelly's sex life?" Sean's tone had deepened to a low and intense pitch as he leaned over the table, making sure I was the only one who could hear him.

Breaking his stare from me, he looked both ways around the restaurant, scoping out the scenery, ensuring that we didn't have a crowd. Fixing his eyes back onto me, he exhaled deeply.

"I hear what you're saying, and I understand truly, but what about me? I'm thirty-four, unmarried, and I have a twenty-one-year-old that I went through hell and back to raise. Do you really think I want to start over again, as a single mom?" I fretted.

Sean bit his bottom lip and rubbed his hands together. He proceeded to shake his head back and forth.

"You think this is hard on you because it may ruin your glamor glitz image, but what about me? I'm the one carrying a baby. I'm the one who will endure the pain of pregnancy. I'm the one who has to deliver a baby while being unsure of the father. ME! Not you or your wife. Take yourself and your reputation out of the center and consider the bigger picture. If this baby isn't yours, I still have to deal with raising the child of a man who raped me!" I shuddered as tears streamed down my face.

In an instant, Sean dashed from his seat and plopped down directly next to me. He pulled me into his embrace, my head resting on his shoulder as I snuggled my face into his arm. I inhaled deeply, breathing in his minty aroma. As he rocked me slowly, soothing my trouble, I whimpered, trying my best to fight back tears and not cause a scene.

"It's okay, Charlie. Let it out. Let it out." He caressed me, his touch everything I needed.

Sean rubbed his large hands into my hair, massaging my scalp as he kissed my forehead. "Don't worry, Charlie, whether the baby belongs to me, you two will be well taken care of," he reassured me with certainty.

"Really, Sean, you mean that?" I marveled.

"You've got my word. Now stop that crying and sit up and talk to me. I want to know everything about the woman who's carrying my child."

Surprised, I lifted my head from his shoulder and turned to face him. He cracked a halfhearted smile, then dabbed his thumb into the corner of my eye and dried my tears.

"So, where did you go to college?" he coolly asked.

"I didn't. I went to a trade school for my LPN, then came to New York for a nursing fellowship with Mercer University."

Sean chuckled. "Mercer University is a college."

"I know smart-ass, but it's not a fancy HBCU like the one Shelly went to and nowhere like Columbia University. And I didn't graduate at the top of my class like you," I defended myself.

"So. You still went to college. Tell me more about your son's father," Sean urged, jumping right in.

I scrunched my lips, cuffing them into my mouth before exhaling slowly. "Jaden's father's name is Aaron. He was a friend of my brother. I was twelve, and he was seventeen."

Sean's eyes bulged as he picked up his glass of water from the other side of the table and gulped it down. "Was he your first love?"

"He was the first boy I had sex with, but far from my first love," I answered matter-of-factly. "He raped me."

Sean kissed his teeth and blew out an agitated breath. "You can't be serious."

"Dead serious. What's worse is that he and another of my brother's friends took turns raping me. Aaron, however, was the stupid one who ejaculated inside of me. I was too young to get an abortion and didn't even know where to get one in Lagrange. So, my parents made me keep the baby and marry him."

Sean was shaking his head profusely as he rubbed the back of his neck.

"You have been through so much and you still walk around with that big smile on your face. I commend you for your strength."

I poked my lips out, irritated by his statement. "This isn't the nineties. Being a strong, black independent woman isn't a badge of honor. It's fucking exhausting. It hurts. It's excruciating, and I'm tired," I bewailed. "Do you have any fucking idea what it's like to be alone? All alone, with no protection? With no one to fall back on? How about having to protect yourself from your own brother and father and not having anyone, not even your own mother, to stand up for you?"

Sean's eyes watered as he held his breath, looking at me and holding on to every word in my mouth. "No," he honestly answered.

"Exactly!" I stressed. "So don't admire me for my strength. Admire God because, without him, I would have caved in a long time ago."

With water dripping from my damp eyes, I wiped my face with the back of my hand. Watching me, Sean picked up a napkin and wiped my face for me again. As he wiped away my cries, a lone tear stained the side of his face. I had never seen a man like him cry. My natural inclination to shield his pain took over as I grabbed him by the sides of his face and looked him deeply in the eyes.

"You're so beautiful in your vulnerability," I expressed to him in a poetic way that felt outer worldly.

As our irises met, Sean softened his simper and leaned into me. The taste of his salty tears brushed against my lips as we softly kissed. He nibbled on my bottom lip a little longer until he whispered four breathy words into my mouth, "I love you, Charlie."

6
MANHOOD
SEAN

I WOKE UP FEELING RESTED AFTER MEETING WITH Charlie. The way we connected yesterday allowed me to express myself in ways I haven't felt free with Shelly. In all the years I have been with Shelly, I have never cried in front of her. Not that I was a mushy kind of nigga anyway with all types of problems that would cause me to cry, but the truth was that Shelly never created a safe space of vulnerability for me to be able to cry if needed or wanted.

Everything in Shelly and our relationship was about her. I spent years chasing her, then winning her back after my slip-up with Gina. Sadly, I spent years putting on the façade as a perfect Superman with a hard exterior and impenetrable stature that I boasted for Shelly. Seeing as I knew how calculated my wife was, everything between us was made up and superficial. One thing was for sure. We were great business partners simply because we were both equally ambitious and competitive.

While Shelly was aesthetically feminine and had the grace and grandeur of a 1940s housewife, she was diplomatically built as a politician. She always had a motive. She spoke with terse, exacting language and had one hell of a poker face. She used her presenting femininity, grace, and her inviting smile to get what she wanted. Being with Shelly was like being with a high-end escort, for it was difficult to ever locate her heart. She was happy as long as the money was coming in and multiplying our position. Well, my position of power was growing, and the sex was racy and consistent.

Still, even when it came to difficult things, like her infertility, Shelly never shared her heart with me or her story. She never explained why she only got her period four times a year or why she never was able to get pregnant by me. Just like everything, she remained in control, controlling me and controlling how much she revealed always created a rift between us. Now, with Charlie pregnant, this was one thing she couldn't control, and somehow it felt like a rebirth.

While I was initially devastated that Charlie was pregnant because I wanted to have my first child with Shelly, my feelings were changing. I was almost forty years old and dying to be a dad, not to mention I was warming up to Charlie. She was accomplished in her own right. She was attractive, although not as beautiful and alluring as Shelly was. Charlie still had her own swag that gave her a unique appeal. Most importantly, I was able to be vulnerable with her. She possessed a softness and quiet strength that I admired and felt safe in.

I wasn't in love with her, but my feelings for her were growing. Being a father and co-parenting with Charlie didn't sound so bad after all. At least I knew she had experience raising a successful son who would soon graduate college. Just the thought of meeting her son and acting as a father figure excited me more.

Lost in my thoughts as I lay next to Shelly in the bed, I rolled over and noticed it was nearly eight o'clock in the morning. Shelly was snoring faintly as I stepped out of bed. It had been months since I went to church and years since Shelly joined me. She wasn't exactly the church-going type of woman. She'd only accompany me if I were attending for business or to make an appearance. Shelly was all about appearances. Other than that, she was a modern woman whose faith in the Lord waned as soon as she became educated and started making loads of money. Shelly ditched Jesus for the universe. She ditched prayer for affirmations and manifestation. She ditched the belief of the supernatural power of healing for self-care and yoga, so I let her have her way and never pressured her about church.

However, I felt like going to church this morning, so I reached for my phone and unhooked it from the charger. As I pulled up my text messages, I saw a kissy face and red heart emoji from Charlie, which made my heart jump. I hadn't felt like a teenage boy in a long time, and it was refreshing. After responding to Charlie, I scrolled down to the group chat with my Omega Psi Phi brothers. I usually kept the notifications off, as the Bruhz were a bit too active in the group, which typically caused distractions from my busy work life. Nonetheless, I always made sure to pop in every once in a while, and I never missed a monthly chapter meeting, unlike Shelly, who just paid her dues and cut checks for Alpha Kappa Alpha's annual slew of fundraisers but never showed her face. I may have been a busy CEO, but I always made time for Que business, and that would never change.

Me: *Thinking about heading to church today. Any bruhz want to meet me at Abyssinian Baptist?*

Seconds later, my message was highlighted with several exclamations and heart emojis.

DirtyDawgQ: *Ehh, I'll pass, but as soon as you find the brunch spot, drop the location.*

Me: *Expected.*

ADPMightyQue: *What time you thinking of rolling out?*

Me: *Service starts at 10, but I want to get there early for some fellowshipping, but any time after 10 is cool.*

ADPMightyQue: *Cool, I'll meet you there.*

OmegaManEsq: *I'm down.*

OmegabyDayQue@Nite: *I'm proud of you, fellas. I don't know the last time I've seen ya asses in church. I'll be there with wifey around 9:30. See you soon.*

Me: *Bet! Let me go and put on my Sunday's Best!*

Excited, I put down my phone and rushed into the bathroom. I had the perfect suit for church, but I was hungrier for the word than anything. As I showered, all I could think about was Charlie. I knew that if she was my woman, we'd be getting ready to go to church together.

A few minutes later, as I lathered my body one more time, the door opened. From the glass shower, I saw Shelly looking well-rested and beautiful as always. It didn't matter what we were going through or what she'd done the night before. She always woke up with a gorgeous morning glow. Sporting a white cami and a thong, her image came closer and closer to the shower until she pulled back the door.

"Morning, baby. You're up early on a Sunday. Where are you going?"

Her eyes danced up and down my wet body until she settled on my face.

"I just woke up in a mood to go to church," I conceded.

As expected, Shelly laughed loudly. "Church? Oh really? What's gotten into you?"

"I'm about to be a father. I just feel like I need to have a private talk with God, and today, I want to do it in the house of the Lord," I defended.

Shelly rolled her eyes. "If you want to have a private talk with God, a loud church full of dissenting spirits isn't the place to go."

"Look, Shelly, I don't want to hear your anti-Christ bullshit today. I'm going to church, and that's that," I declared and swiftly slid the shower door back.

Entering Abyssinian Baptist brought back so many memories of my father. Founded in 1808 and led by the late and great Adam Clayton Powell and his son Adam Clayton Powell Jr, Abyssinian Baptist was instrumental in the desegregation of churches and in the Black Power movements during the 1900s. Although it was obvious that the church was adopting some modern ways, through the presence of cameramen operating sturdy production equipment to record service for the online stream, the church's interior only had a slight facelift.

Inside of the church still resembled the classic Baptist layout with a ship-shaped nave that extended to the altar, several wooden pews, and a decorative pulpit that sat high on top of the baptistry. I was almost certain they still conducted baptisms after service. Ushers were dressed in white and lined up along the aisle while the choir was adorned with burgundy cloaks as they sang. There was also a line of praise dancers dancing to the music in front of the pulpit.

While I tried my best not to get emotional, the spirit moved me so much that I felt my eyes getting wet. I was about to be a father. I had so many mixed emotions, from elation to confusion and disappointment. I vowed never to have a child out of wedlock, yet here I was, breaking my vow to my father. If he were still alive, he'd be more than disappointed. Once on the upper level of the church, I noticed two of my frat brothers seated to the left. As I approached, they both stood up.

"My man! You looking sharp," Percy, one of the tallest brothers I know, standing at six-foot-seven, complimented as he dapped me up and pulled me into his embrace. We exchanged grips, ensuring we concealed our secret handshake.

"Ahh, thanks, can't complain. I'm feeling good," I responded as I scooted over and dapped up Diesel, who was the complete opposite of his name.

Short, pudgy, and stout, Diesel had impeccable swag and a way with the ladies. He knew how to laugh the draws off the most uptight chick of the bunch. I'd seen it many times with my own eyes over the years.

"Where's wifey?" I asked D after we exchanged grips as well.

"When I told her we were meeting, she ditched me for a spa day with the ladies. How's Shelly?"

"You know Shelly, she ain't stepping foot inside a church."

"Same ole, Shelly," Diesel added in.

I nodded my head and chuckled. "Yeah, same ole Shelly."

For the next two hours, we were wrapped in a nostalgic bubble, yet we were experiencing reality. Abyssinian hadn't changed one bit. After enduring the opera-esque praise and worship, the heavy-laden praise dancing, and the discombobulated message that contained all three scriptures, if that, my head was spinning. Diesel, Percy, and I left immediately after service, and I was grateful.

"I hate to say it, but we need a more modern church to attend!" I declared as we sat at the bar at Red Rooster. Brunch was in full bloom, but the music was set at a comfortable volume, perfect for us to talk.

"You're right! It's just that church holds so much rich history. I can't see myself tithing elsewhere," Percy added.

"I hear you, but I can't see myself going there again." I laughed. Diesel joined in, letting out a low hackle.

"Wifey and I are still members at CCC out in Brooklyn. From time to time, we frequent Abyssinian, but it's been months," Diesel stated. "Anyway, congrats on the partnership with the Koch Foundation, man.

I'm proud of you!"

"We're all proud of you. Our bruh is a big-time CEO of one of the biggest hospitals in the city, following right behind your pops but doing it bigger. A round of drinks on me!" Percy added. "My man, get us all a round of rum and Coke!" he shouted across the bar to the young white male bartender.

The bartender nodded to show his acknowledgment and started to prepare our drinks.

"Thank you. I couldn't have done this without the Bruhz support."

"Yeah, yeah, we alright, but them Mason brothers hold real weight. I know they were able to shake the table for you," Diesel added in.

"For sure. It pays to be a Mason. My grandmaster was able to put a good word into the board, which really went a long way, even longer than my father's legacy. For some reason, I thought that my father's reputation alone would propel me to the next level, but it was really my grandmaster, and for that, I'm thankful. Still, I know you guys were praying and interceding for me, and that's just as powerful."

"To brotherhood!" Percy declared, picking up the glass the bartender had laid out in front of us.

"To manhood!" Diesel blurted out, correcting us.

"To MANHOOD!" we all repeated in unison and clanked our glasses together.

After taking a swoosh and allowing it to settle down my throat, we all let out a sigh.

"So, what's new, D?" Percy asked, nudging his head in my direction.

They called me D instead of Sean. We had five other guys with the name Sean in our chapter.

"Well, I do have something to tell y'all niggas."

Diesel chuckled. "I figured your ass did. It's not often you write in the chat that you wanna meet up at church. We knew something was up."

I chuckled, revealing a sly grin. "Y'all know me too well."

"You damn right," Percy interjected. "So wassup, nigguh!"

I took a large swig of my drink and allowed it to burn my throat before biting my bottom lip.

"Let it out nigguh!" Percy egged, exaggerating his nearly exasperated southern drawl.

I scooted back on the bar stool and looked back and forth between both of them. "I'm gon' be a father."

Percy and Diesel's face lit up. Percy folded his burly arms, almost suffocating his chest, and bounced his head with a satisfying grin on his face. Diesel held out his hand, forcefully dapped me up and aggressively pulled me into an embrace. He patted my back twice and held me a bit tight before letting me go.

"Congratulations to you and wifey. I'm so happy for y'all. Just a warning: those man cave days are about to be over. Trust me!" Diesel added.

"I wish you guys a speedy pregnancy and a safe delivery," Percy said.

"I second the speedy pregnancy. That's the most aggravating part.

When she's pregnant, you're pregnant. You start getting the symptoms and the cravings. And if you don't watch out, you'll pack on some weight, too," Diesel shared. "I gained thirty pounds when Tina had our twins," he stated.

"Damn, I think I remember that. You were all extra stocky and shit," Percy ragged.

Something in me wanted to join in their happiness and well wishes for Shelly's pregnancy. Perhaps if I joined in, I could conceal the truth and make myself feel better about the uncertain reality, but these were my brothers. I needed them. I needed their advice, so I couldn't lie or withhold information.

"Shelly isn't pregnant," I muttered.

Both of the guy's chatter ceased, and an uncomfortable eerie silence dawned over us.

Percy picked up his glass and drank the last remnants before shooing over the bartender. "Boss man, can we get another round?"

"Sure. Same thing?"

"Yeah, rum and Coke, but this time Wray & Nephew," Percy requested. "We need something strong!"

Diesel stepped back and looked me up and down. "Damn, man. I thought you were one of the last good Bruhz left. You disappoint me!" He joked and burst into laughter that he ceased several seconds later. "Come here, bro. It's all good." He followed up with his arms open.

I kissed my teeth and laughed at Diesel's theatrics. "I didn't cheat, exactly. And besides, I'm embarrassed to say Shelly already knows about it."

"Well, just let it out, nigguh. If Shelly already knows, what's the fear for?" Percy asked.

"Shelly and I have a girlfriend. Throughout the years, we have had several."

Percy and Diesel's eyes bulged.

"So, you guys are swingers?" Diesel asked, confused.

"No, they're poly. Swingers are generally couples where both parties are bi-sexual. The men have sex with the men, too."

"Ehh," we all groaned.

"What D is describing is a polyamorous relationship. He and his wife have a girlfriend that only belongs to them. Am I right?" Percy asked for clarification.

I nodded in agreement. "Yes, but this has never been my thing. It's Shelly's thing. She loves women."

"Can you blame her?" Diesel loudly wailed.

My chin locked, and a hostile smug crept up my face. "Yeah, I can. Because now I'm having a child with a woman who's not my wife," I snapped.

A hissing sound rolled out of Percy's mouth as he placed his hand on my shoulder. "Yeah, no man wants to have a baby by a woman he's not in love with."

"Exactly, but it's not just that. The woman is cool for the most part, and I find myself growing closer to her. Meanwhile, Shelly and I aren't in the best place right now," I explained.

"Damnnnnnn, my boy. Trouble in paradise for real. How far along is she?" Diesel asked.

"We just found out, so I'm assuming she's early. She's definitely not showing, but we haven't even been to the doctor yet."

"Well, are y'all thinking about keeping it?" Percy questioned with raised eyebrows. "It may be early enough for a quick abortion pill," he suggested.

Just the sound of the word abortion pained me. With grave seriousness, I scrunched my nose and looked at both of them. "Shelly has never even gotten pregnant by me. I can't kill my first baby. I'm about to turn forty and have nobody to pass my legacy down to." My voice was shattering as my throat clogged up.

"I understand, D, and you're right. As a man, all you have is your word and your legacy. Without both, life feels incomplete. I say have the baby and make it work with Shelly. She's already cool with it, so this baby should bring you closer, not tear you apart," Diesel advised with sincerity, his left eye raised.

I let out a loud sigh and felt a tear roll down the side of my face.

Percy yoked me up from the bar stool and hugged me tightly as he patted my back. "It's all good, bruh. Don't worry. We got you."

7

HER

SHELLY

FEELINGS OF INFERIORITY AND DISCONTENT BOM-barded my mind, causing a tightness in my chest as I thought about what the next few hours would bring. Briskly walking ahead of Sean and Charlie, who were enthralled in what seemed like an interesting conversation, I opened the door to an office building on the Upper West Side of Manhattan.

"Thanks, Shelly," Charlie stated as she walked in first. Sean followed behind her, completely avoiding chatter or eye contact with me.

Exquisitely boasting a beautiful, vaulted ceiling, polished marble floors, and ornamental gold metalwork and mosaics, we were standing in one of the grandest lobbies in New York City.

"Seriously though, that had to be the funniest shit I'd seen in a long time," Sean yakked in Charlie's direction.

"You're a fool." Charlie chuckled as she pressed the button for the elevator.

"I wasn't aware you were a comedian, babe," I chided, gazing directly into Sean's eyes.

"Sometimes I am. You'd notice if we didn't spend all our time talking about business or fucking!"

Appalled by his response, I gasped, then quickly swallowed my humiliation. Things were just getting worse between Sean and me. Since finding out that Charlie was pregnant a few weeks ago, it seemed like he was warming up to her, yet his heart was as cold as an icebox for me.

A quick glance at Charlie revealed she was as uncomfortable as I was. We stepped inside the elevator one by one and remained silent as we shot up to the sixteenth floor.

As we entered the private doctor's office, hints of lavender and disinfectant solution invaded my nostrils. Concealed on the last floor in the building, this was the perfect location, one that really put the private in private doctor. I was almost sure that we wouldn't be seen by any of our staff, at the least. Apparently, this doctor saw many high-profile clients, including celebrities and politicians. Serious about not being spotted, I adorned my face with the darkest Dior shades I had in my closet. A silk leopard print scarf was wrapped tightly around my head, coddling my neck. To further seal the deal, I pulled the brim of my bucket hat down, covering my forehead. Although slightly gaudy, my get-up complimented the misty fog and chilly rain that dawned on the city.

I approached the receptionist's desk quickly. Before I could garner the receptionist's attention, Sean grabbed my arm.

"Take a seat, Shelly. Let Charlie and I handle this," he declared as he pulled me to the side.

Appalled, I jumped back and watched my husband and our girlfriend mosey up to the front desk. As Charlie introduced herself, Sean's hand glided down the small of her back. He rested his hand gently on her lower back and turned his head to the side, softness and care fuddled in the gaze of his eyes as he held onto every word Charlie uttered.

He used to look at me like that.

As pressure welled up in my heart, I motioned backward, taking a seat in the chair. After they finished signing in, the two of them sat in seats directly across from me. Cozied up together, Sean turned his body toward her, making sure to avoid any contact with me. We've been disconnected for weeks. He barely spoke to me. He didn't cuddle me in bed, and it's been a while since we've had breakfast together. Coffee and commotion was what we called it. While sipping coffee, we discussed our plans for the day and all the chaos at the hospital. It was our daily ritual, but these last few weeks, Sean was up and dressed by the time I made my way out of bed. He didn't wake me like usual, and he was gone and hadn't even left me any coffee to drink by the time I entered the kitchen.

Instead of pressing the issue, I let it continue for several days. Sean knew I was a master power player and that I wouldn't address him. He'd need to be a man and come forth with his issues. Besides, I still had a hospital to run. As much as I loved Sean, I refused to let his bullshit bring me down, mentally or emotionally. Self-preservation has always been my priority.

I sat back in my seat, crossed my legs, and adjusted my posture, executing my signature high-power pose. Lowering my eyes, I watched them closely. Charlie was so lost in the attention Sean was giving her that she barely noticed me, but it wasn't her fault, and I wasn't mad at her. With her past, she never had a good man in her life. She ought to be thankful that I allowed her to borrow Sean. Rocking my foot back and forth, a sly smirk crept up my lip as I regained my confidence.

You have nothing to worry about, Shellz. She may be having his baby, but you're the wife, and that holds a hell of a lot more weight.

"Ms. Thompson, you're eight weeks pregnant," the Asian ultrasound tech announced as she pointed to the projector.

Charlie covered her mouth with her hands, holding her gasp in. "Oh my god, look at our baby!" she gushed as she turned to face Sean and me.

Instantaneously, Sean got up from his seat, went to her side, and grabbed her hand in his. His dimples appeared as the brow lines around his mouth formed. A soft grin crept up his face, reminding me of the same happy simper he looked at me with on our wedding day: bliss and joy. As Sean and Charlie stared into each other's eyes, forgetting that I was even in the room, my heart began to sink into the pits of my soul.

For some reason, I *thought* I had it in me. I *thought* that I could study the sonogram without any ounce of discomfort. I *thought* I was built like a bulletproof No Limit solider and that watching Sean fan out over his unborn child would be a breeze. I *thought* it wouldn't hurt me, but as the entire room, including Charlie, Sean, and the ultrasound tech, ooh'd and ahh'd at the sight of the features forming behind a gray scale filter on the projector, I felt like I was hit by an eighteen-wheeler.

Stiffness encapsulated me. My belly throbbed, swollen with horror, until I just couldn't take it anymore. Their happiness was infectiously dreadful, causing my entire body to ache. Even the sounds of my thumping heart didn't cause them to inquire why I had suddenly got up. Holding back tears, I rose from my seat, scurried toward the door, and slipped out of the room. Sadly, by the time I exited the building and retrieved my car from the valet, I hadn't received a single call or text. I could just feel my hold on Sean slipping away. *He didn't love me anymore.*

"Arrgh!" I screamed at the top of my lungs once I got into my car.

I whacked my steering wheel several times, causing the horn to beep loudly. The Hispanic valet attendee stared at me bizarrely, with his hands spread out. I sneered at him before whipping my phone out and heading to the App Store. I downloaded Her and Lex, two of my favorite lesbian dating apps. I deleted them over a year ago when I recommitted myself to Sean. At the end of 2021, I made up my mind that if my and Sean's relationship were going to last, I'd have to give up my desire for women.

Deleting the apps made it easier to focus on my marriage and fall back in love with Sean. I thought I was truly done surfing the net for random women to hook up with, but considering that I was texting a wild ex-lover, I knew I was at my lowest. A tear trickled down the side of my face as Izzy sent me her location. I took a deep breath as I drove off in the direction of her condo. As much as I knew I shouldn't have, seeing her would help me escape everything, causing me heartache.

Forty minutes later, I made it to her condo. I met Isabelle Lorde Rollins, a bi-racial OB/GYN on Her, a few years ago. While she was a prestigious doctor who won several awards for her groundbreaking research and unprecedented practices, she was truly just a mess of a cokehead. As soon as Izzy opened the door, it was evident that not only was she still using, but that she was high as hell. Seeing as her meticulously, minimally clad condo reeked of weed smoke, I wasn't sure if she was high off of just weed or her lethal combination of weed, coke, and booze.

Holding a blunt to her mouth, she took a long pull before blowing the smoke in my face. "I didn't think I'd ever see you again, Shelly." She snickered.

"I'm just as shocked as you," I sassed, smacking my lips together.

"Don't do that. You know how much those lips drive me crazy." Izzy was the most forward woman I met.

Twirling my tongue across my top lip, I smirked, looking Izzy straight in the eyes. She was still naturally beautiful with that soft hair I loved rubbing my fingers through. Nonetheless, her beady eyes and dry skin told me that she was as depressed and tired as I was.

"Relax. We have enough time for that. Catch me up first. How have things been?"

Izzy sucked her teeth loudly. "Now you know damn well you didn't download Her again and hit me up to talk. Let's not act like we truly care about how each other is doing," she declared crassly, without an ounce of concern.

"But I do care."

Sucking on her blunt again, Izzy inhaled, then exhaled a large puff of smoke. "Besides the fact that my ex died over a year ago and I'm on probation from work, things are going just fine. How the hell are you?" she sarcastically asked.

"Damn, Izzy, I'm so sorry to hear about Sam. How have you been holding up?" I asked sincerely.

With a pestering smirk, Izzy sighed, "Last time I checked, you were the CNO of Presbyterian Hospital, not a therapist. Read the room, baby girl, just like I'm doing with you. Let's be honest. I haven't heard from you in at least two years, so I'm certain it's trouble in paradise. Sean's probably cheating, but that's neither here nor there. Now, come and take a few lines to ease your mind," Izzy jested as she walked over to her couch, where a glass end table sat with a heap of cocaine on it.

Sitting on the couch, she separated some coke on a magazine and began cutting it into lines with a steel-edged razor blade. In a matter of two minutes, she used a straw to devour two of the seven lines of coke she had prepared.

"Damn, that's good!" she shouted as she faced me. "Come on, what you're waiting for? Let's get this party started."

Hesitantly, I dug my back deeper into the couch.

"Don't be shy, girl," Izzy teased.

Fidgeting, I shook my head back and forth. "Izzy, I haven't done coke in years. I don't know," I panted indecisively.

"Quit playing, girl," Izzy said as she grabbed me by the wrists closer to the end table. She passed me a straw and crinkled her brows. "Let's go!"

Nervously, I snatched the straw out of her hand and leaned over the glass end table. Raising one end of the straw to my nose and the other onto the line of coke, I snorted, and within ten seconds, the substance rushed to my brain, spiking my dopamine levels through the roof. I came up for air, vision glossy and my cheekbones raised.

"Good, right?" Izzy questioned.

Giddy, I nodded, bouncing like a bobblehead. "Yeah, I want more!"

Izzy chuckled as she kissed her teeth. "Do your thing, baby girl. You can have whatever you like."

And so I did. Line after line, I snorted, enjoying the various highs I traveled to until Izzy and I rolled around her floor, licking alcohol off each other's bodies. As our pussy lips glided and slipped and slid against each other, sensation traveled through my veins. Izzy was a scissoring queen, and from the combination of the coke and the sex, I was flying higher than the Kingda Ka at Six Flags. This was the first time in a long time that I truly felt alive. I felt free with Izzy.

Unleashing my inhibitions, I climbed on top of Izzy, leaning over to the glass end table, and snorted two more lines back-to-back. I was floating so high that I pounced down on Izzy, kissing her deeply and passionately, ravishing her body, massaging my left palm in her scalp, and gripping her right ass cheek with the other hand. I felt so in control, as I loved to dominate studs, just like Izzy. It gave me a rush, a sensational rush that felt so good, so freeing and so damn secure, until my vision went blank, and I couldn't feel or see a damn thing.

62

8

CRASH OUT

RODNEY KANE

"*LOOK, MAN, I'VE PAID YOU TWICE ALREADY, AND you still don't have an address for me!*" I barked, spit flying out of my mouth as I yelled at the useless private investigator I'd hired to help track down Charlie.

The middle-aged white guy, who couldn't have been taller than five-foot-three, leaned forward, fear all over his face. "You didn't hire me to give you the address of one of the most powerful men in New York." Stuttering, the PI twiddled his fidgety hands and tried not to stare too hard at my beat-up face.

Since I was released from the hospital, I had several stitches alongside my face, a busted lip that hadn't fully healed, and dark bruises under my eyes that I wasn't sure would fade.

"You hired me to find Charlie."

"But you haven't done that yet, either," I stressed.

The PI rattled his hands, pushing them forward as if to ward me off. "But I do have some very important information for you."

Lowering my eyes, I stared at him coldly. "Spit it the fuck out, then."

Digging into his bag, he pulled out a manila folder and placed it onto the table that separated us as we sat in a busy Starbucks on E57th Street in Manhattan. He opened the folder and there was a picture of Charlie and that bitch ass nigga Sean. They were walking hand in hand out of some fancy ass building. The PI removed the photo to reveal another picture of Sean opening the passenger seat of his car for Charlie to get inside.

"When was this?"

"Two days ago," the PI answered. "Although the date isn't important. The where is." The PI's eyes lit up. "They were leaving an OB/GYN's office on the Upper West Side. Dr. Seltser is the gynecologist for many celebs who have conceived and given birth in New York. After a bit of digging and paying the receptionist fifteen hundred dollars, I was able to find out that Charlie is eight weeks pregnant."

I swallowed hard, and my eyes shot open wide. "Are you serious?"

The PI picked up the manila folder and skimmed through it before pulling out a few papers. "Here's a copy of her sonogram, and a confirmation of her blood tests that confirms her pregnancy."

Holding the documents in my hand, I studied them so long, my hands started shaking. Even my eyes watered. "I'm going to be a father," I whimpered, unable to control the tears coming from my eyes.

The PI stared at me wildly and crunched his lips together. "How are you so sure this is your baby?"

Fuming, I couldn't believe he asked me some stupid shit like that. "Nigga, don't question me. I know because I know, and that's not even your concern. Seeing as you weren't clear about my requests, let me make it crystal this time around. Get me the address to Sean Fox's home the next time I see you!" I barked.

The PI cleared his throat and raised his brow. "You couldn't pay me enough to do that. No malice will fall back on me. He's too powerful to go after without serving jail time, and I'm not made like you. Now what I can do is get you the address to Charlie's friend Sade's house because that's where she's been staying."

I leaned forward and grabbed his collar so tightly. I didn't care about the stares that shot my way from the coffee drinkers in Starbucks. "I'm not paying you for shit I already know. Sade lives in Roosevelt Projects. I'm paying you for information that's hard to get, but I see I'll have to use my own resources. Thanks for the info, but I won't be needing your services anymore," I growled before letting him go and snatching the documents and folder off the table.

As I got up from my seat, all eyes were on me, but I didn't give one fuck.

"What the fuck are you nosy motherfuckers looking at? Drink your coffee and mind your fucking business!" I raged before storming off, leaving that useless bastard shaking with terror.

"Damn, my nigga, it's been a few weeks since you got stitched up, and you still look like shit," Relly, my day one, I used to roll with from Albany Projects bantered. Although I was from Harlem, I fucked with a lot of Brooklyn cats.

"Nigga, don't watch me. Watch TV. Why the fuck you preeing the next man's face for, anyway?" I threw back, challenging him.

"Here you go with the extra shit, nigga. It's not hard to notice when you over here in my face with that shit on your lip," he wailed, laughing out loud and pointing at me.

It was early April, the first few weeks of spring, and the sun was shining. The high was set at seventy degrees, with just enough sun and a cool breeze. All the bitches were outside prancing around in their old summer gear from last year. Stick figures were sporting fat asses, wigs, and eyelashes as they held ice cups in their hand and pretended not to hear our whistles and "Hey ma" greetings. As we sat on top of the benches, the heel of our construction boots plastered on the engraved chess board on the concrete table, we both turned our heads once we saw a gang of pigs walk through the courtyard.

"Niggas can't have one day without the fucking NYPD trying to fuck it up. The hood just ain't the same no more," I complained, disregarding Relly's earlier comment.

Relly, who was taller and five years older than me, sighed and sucked his teeth. "Exactly, the hood ain't home for niggas like us anymore. That's why I got the fuck up out of here and just passed through on the humble to see my sister and my nieces and nephews. As soon as Taina got pregnant, I knew I couldn't raise my kids out here," he grunted.

I inhaled deeply and exhaled an aggravated breath. "Yeah nigga, I know because Queens is so much better than Brooklyn," I taunted.

"Y'all niggas get a little older and swear moving to Queens provides a better life as if it ain't killers rampant on the Southside. Man, the same shit happening out here is going on out there!"

"Nah, nigga it ain't. Besides, I don't live on the Southside, and you know that. My kids go to a good school. Taina and I are on the school board. We attend community board meetings and all. Shit is really different," he boldly asserted as he folded his arms in defense.

"Man, whatever. Springfield ain't your community. This is your community, and you could have easily been on the school and community board out here as well. You just chose to abandon your neighborhood."

Relly hopped off the top of the bench. Anger rushed to his face. "Nigga, don't throw stones when you live in a glass house, and if you got a glass jaw, you should watch your mouth. I would say I'd break your face, but somebody already did that."

I laughed wildly at his boldness. "Niggas move to Queens and think they're 50 Cent. You a clown ass nigga."

"Nah, nigga, you're the clown. Don't make me cut yo' ass and pack you the fuck up. C'mon, son. Look at you. Face fucked up. You ain't got no whip, no bitch, and no breesh. I'm not the one you should be arguing with. Them niggas that fucked you up need to be getting the smoke you directing to me. Chill the fuck out, my guy."

Now, I had jumped off the table and was on his ass like white on rice. Face to face, I snarled, crunching my brows, and hardening my face.

"Nigga, ain't nobody scared of you just cause you got them scars and wounds," he hissed, his hot breath on my face.

Staring into the blacks of his pupils, I balled my fists up and locked my jaw. Relly's nose was up, and his nostrils flared as he looked down on me. I don't know what came over me, but my eyes watered and soon tears were streaming down my face. Relly grabbed me into a forceful hug, patting the back of my head.

"C'mon, my nigga, don't cry out here. You good, bro."

For some reason, his words, which I'm certain were meant to be comforting, actually caused me to bawl louder. Fortunately, my cries were muffled as I buried my face in his shirt. Relly continued patting me on the back as he shook his head back and forth. As soon as I got myself together, I wiggled out of his embrace, head down and shoulders drooping, embarrassed to look at him.

"Look, my nigga, my bad for coming at you crazy, but the truth of the matter is that shit is not looking too good for you now, but that doesn't mean you can't change it. And if it makes you feel any better, I can send out a call for them niggas that got at you. You said them niggas were some Harlem Bloods, right?" he asked, concern heaving through his throat.

Whimpering and drying my eyes, I nodded my head in agreement. I couldn't piece together the connection for weeks, especially since I was healing, but it all came to me suddenly.

"Harlem Bloods carried out the job, but I think I know who was behind it!"

Bug-eyed, Relly flinched to signal my attention. "Who, nigga?"

"That bitch ass nigga Sean, the CEO at the hospital Charlie works for."

Relly scratched his chin, then folded his arms under his chest. "Nigga, you're bugging. Why the fuck would he be behind some street shit like this?"

Contemplating on whether to come clean, I finally gave in. If I was going to go after Sean, I needed an army, which meant I had to be honest. "When I couldn't find Charlie, I went to her job and cornered her boss, trying to get answers from her. I pulled out a box cutter on the bitch."

Disappointment painted Relly's face as he pulled a neatly rolled spliff from behind his ear and lit it. After taking a long pull, he exhaled slowly before saying, "You're a wild boy, my nigga. You're a wild boy."

9

IN SYNC

CHARLIE

"**W**HERE THE FUCK COULD SHE BE? IT'S BEEN three days, and she hasn't answered the phone. I'm starting to get worried," I fretted, throwing my head onto Sean's chest as we snuggled up on the couch.

Sean pulled me tighter into his embrace and gently rocked me. I leaned up and kissed him on the cheek, nuzzling my nose against his chin, hoping to comfort him. If I was worried about Shelly's disappearance, I knew it was eating him up.

"The only good thing about her being gone this long is that now we can finally file a missing person's report," Sean said, his voice low and eyes fixated on an invisible space in the air.

I could sense that he was hurting, which made me hug him tighter. Resting my head on his chest, I traced my finger against the fast-beating rhythm of his heart. "I'm so sorry, baby. Do you think the ultrasound set her off?"

"I don't see why. Shelly has never gotten pregnant by me to even lose a baby to be triggered by seeing a sonogram. She acts like she's not interested in having children, anyway."

I remained quiet, allowing Sean's words to marinate. It was clear he didn't know about Shelly's infertility issues unless he would have understood why my pregnancy was triggering to her. Although, it came as a surprise to me also, seeing as Shelly was in support of my pregnancy from the beginning, being that I knew her story and the fact that she was an emotional creature just like me, it all started to make sense. Shelly wasn't envious or jealous of Sean and me. She was saddened by the fact that my pregnancy reminded her of her barren womb.

I let out a shuddered breath and rubbed my hands along Sean's leg. All I could do was comfort him, and I knew I didn't have to say much to do so. Simply being there was enough, not to mention I wouldn't dare betray Shelly's trust by telling him her secret, and I didn't have it in me to hurt Sean more than he was already hurting. As the third party, I found myself doing what was necessary to shield them both. At first, when I agreed to this arrangement, it was all fun, orgasms, and shopping sprees, but it never occurred to me how much responsibility I held. Being in a polyamorous relationship meant that I had two people to consider. My loyalty was split between both of them, which meant that I had to use my discernment wisely to make the best decisions for the overall union.

In no way did I want to cause a rift between Shelly and Sean. I enjoyed being with both of them and even though Sean and I were growing closer, I still didn't forget how quickly he discarded me when he first found out I was pregnant. In fact, I still didn't fully trust him. It was Shelly who I knew more, so her disappearance was killing me softly.

She had this quiet strength about her that I was looking forward to leaning on during this pregnancy. It was our friendship and the trust we built over the years that made me comfortable enough with even succumbing to this relationship. To fathom that I may never see her again was just too much to bear.

As I continued to sit quietly, just hearing the beating of Sean's heart, I broke the ice and asked him one question. "Do you think filing a missing person's report will help us find her?"

Sean grunted as he pulled me closer and proceeded to repeatedly bounce his leg. "No. I don't. With my profile, going to the police will just expose us. Within six hours of reporting or even less, my phone will be ringing nonstop from the board, donors, the press, my executive staff, my frat brothers, my Masonic brothers, Shelly's line sisters, and even my estranged family in Barbados will find a way to pry into my business, our business," Sean fretted.

"Baby, don't look at it like that. The more you're exposed, the quicker and easier it will be to find Shelly," I countered, offering compassion.

Sean abruptly pulled away from me for the first time in days. I was enjoying the extra affection and attention he'd recently extended to me. Sean had opened up even more after finding out I was eight weeks pregnant. His loving and caring side, which he usually kept to a limit with me, was being lifted. I guess now that he knew there was a possibility that I was carrying his baby made him more empathetic to me. Yet when he pulled away, it reminded me of how cold he could be.

"Logically, that makes sense, but realistically it doesn't. Reporting this will only expose our polyamorous affairs and the fact that you're pregnant, and I just don't need that kind of heat. This partnership with the Koch Foundation means everything to me. Although the check has been deposited and funds have already been allocated and spent, that doesn't mean they can't recant their sponsorship and demand their money back. I just have too much to lose," Sean protested.

Anger and irritation wrestled back and forth between my ears as I tried my hardest to conceal them and maintain my composure, but Sean was starting to piss me off. "Forgive me, Mr. CEO, but you're not the only one with much to lose. I still have a job to return to. This affects me as much as it affects you. For once, think about someone other than your fucking self. What about your wife, who is God knows where?" I asserted.

Getting up from my seat, I stood directly in front of Sean, who sat on the couch with his elbows on his knees. His wrinkled forehead told it all. He may have tried to play it cool, but he was stressed as fuck.

"Look, fuck what the public, the press, or your donors will think. The main important thing should be locating Shelly!"

Bouncing his head steadily, he avoided eye contact with me, and instead, his gaze pierced right through me. It appeared as if he was in a completely different dimension.

"Sean!" I shouted.

Without saying a word, he stood up and finally faced me. Grabbing me into his arms, he peered down at me, his eyes heavy and wet. "You're right, baby. You're right."

Swallowing hard and inhaling deeply, he exhaled out of his nose, and his breath settled on my face. We were so close that I felt like I was in his skin. I felt like I could feel and hear everything he was trying to process.

"I'm scared as much as you. I have a baby growing in me, a crazy ex-boyfriend, and an adult son coming home soon. This isn't by any means easy for me, either. Imagine the scrutiny that will come with this for me, but one thing I know is that I can't go through this pregnancy without Shelly. I need her as much as I need you."

Sean's simper softened as a lone tear streamed down the side of his face. "I know, baby, I know because I need her too."

I smiled, then raised my hand to his face and wiped his eyes. Sean wrapped his large arms around me, and I stood on my tippy toes to kiss him. I could taste the salt from his tears, but I didn't care. I just wanted him to know that I wasn't going anywhere.

"First thing in the morning, we'll go to the precinct. Tonight, I can't deal with that. All I want is some alone time with you and my baby."

His need for me turned me on and made me feel safe and wanted.

"And all I want is to be right next to you."

"I'm going to order some pizza and wings. What flavor wings and pizza do you want?" Sean asked a few hours later.

"Sweet and sour wings and a thin crust pepperoni pie. Add some cinnamon sticks and a Ginger Ale," I answered without looking at him.

We were so enthralled in *Law & Order SVU*. The USA network has been paying homage to Munch since Richard Belzer recently passed away. We had to be on our seventh episode, so I'm pretty sure it was after midnight.

Sean didn't respond and instead just stared at me in awe.

"What, babe?"

Shaking his head back and forth, he smiled at me. "That's exactly what I planned to order for me, minus the cinnamon sticks. Thin-crust pepperoni is my favorite pizza, and Ginger Ale is the only soda I drink. Now, this is the real test. Canada Dry or Schweppes?" he asked with a ring of enthusiasm in his voice.

"Neither, unless it's Raspberry Schweppes, but personally, I'd prefer Seagram's," I answered matter-of-factly.

Sean chuckled softly. "Wow, I can't believe we have so much in common. I'll be sure to get Seagram's and the Raspberry Schweppes. Ice cream?"

"Butter Pecan," I answered.

"Perfect," he whispered before kissing me on the lips.

As Sean threw on a jogger suit and some sneakers, I couldn't help but think about what he said. Outside of food, we really did have a lot in common. After spending the entire afternoon talking, I discovered we enjoyed the same TV shows. Our two favorites of all time being *Law & Order: SVU* and *The Boondocks*. Both of our favorite colors were blue, and our all-time favorite vacation spot was Aruba because of the breathtaking pink sand on Flamingo Beach. We both loved R&B music and preferred Anthony Hamilton over Musiq Soulchild. It felt like we spent years talking and learning about each other, something we should have done before we became intimate, but better late than never was my motto.

"I'll be back soon, babe. Don't fall asleep on me," he warned while motioning toward the door.

"I won't. I'll be right here waiting for you when you get back," I assured.

Once Sean returned, we were both so turned on that we forgot all about the food he scrounged from the streets of Harlem, and we made sweet love — slow, long, and fulfilling. We both came in unison and fell asleep, never breaking our embrace or separating his shaft from my love canal.

I couldn't believe it, but I was falling for Mr. Desean Fox, and if I wasn't mistaken, he was already in love with me too.

10
EPIPHANY
SEAN

PULLING MY ARM FROM UNDER CHARLIE, ENSURING I didn't wake her, I couldn't help but dread the day ahead of me. For the last few months, things have been going so well at work. Not only would I contribute that to the partnership with the Koch Foundation, but my team was gelling together pretty well after I let a few people go and brought a few others on board. This shit with Shelly would sure put a dent in all the hard work I put in and the progress I'd made with the hospital. Nothing was worse than a scandal, for it held the power to change a lot and attract unnecessary attention, but Charlie was right. We had to find Shelly. Despite how much I hated Shelly right now for putting us in this predicament, I was truly worried.

Disappearing and going missing for days on end was not like Shelly at all. This was a woman I had known for over fifteen years, yet suddenly I felt like I didn't know her at all because I would have never suspected this. As I paced back and forth in the bathroom, my anger began to wane, melting into neurotic concern. *Where the fuck was my wife?*

Approaching the sink, I peered at myself in the mirror. Wrinkle lines accompanied my forehead, and there were small heat bumps saturated on my right cheek. Stressed was an understatement. I was silently losing my shit yet having Charlie by my side kept me together. Just the thought that I had a seed on the way gave me a new perspective on everything. I had to think smart and make the best moves as the leader of this family. As these thoughts bombarded my mind, I cut on the faucet and splashed water on my skin. The cold water cooled me down and revitalized me. With a new spirit, I reached for my phone and dialed Shelly's number, hoping she would answer. To no avail, it went straight to voicemail again without even ringing.

"FUCK!" I screamed, then covered my mouth, hoping I didn't disturb Charlie and the baby.

Before I could even regain my composure, my loud ringtone blared through the room. It was the New York Presbyterian Hospital's main line. Nobody ever called me from the main line. If it were an emergency, someone from my executive staff would have called me on my work phone.

Who the fuck could be calling me from there?

I took a deep breath and then answered. "Sean Fox speaking,"

"Yes, hello, Mr. Fox. My name is Ashley Ellen, and I am a patient intake coordinator at New York Presbyterian Hospital. I am calling to notify you that your wife, Shenelle Fox, was admitted last night for acute cocaine toxicity and is currently being treated. She has been revived and is doing well enough to have visitors."

Listening to her every word caused my face to tighten and my blood to boil. "Ashley, you do know that I am the CEO of New York Presbyterian, and Shenelle is the CNO. There's no way my wife overdosed on cocaine. She doesn't use drugs."

Ashely cleared her throat and inhaled so deeply I could hear her windpipe rattle. "Yes, Mr. Fox, I am well aware. While we have never met, I am familiar with you and your wife as I have seen many photos of both of you. I know this may be hard to hear, but we are one hundred percent certain that the patient admitted is your wife, Shenelle Fox."

I couldn't believe her. It just didn't make any sense. Besides mushrooms, Shelly and I have never done drugs. I have also never suspected that she did coke. Shit, we don't even smoke weed. What the fuck was happening?

"You said you admitted her last night, so why the hell am I just hearing about this today? And why am I hearing it from you and not a member of my executive team?" I roared. Now I was pissed. Why the fuck hadn't I been the first person notified as soon as she came through those doors? And where the fuck was my assistant Chacha?

"Uh, I believe the patient intake coordinator who works the graveyard shift called you several times last night. Hold on," she mumbled.

Keystrokes from what sounded like a computer rattled in my ear. Shortly after, she returned.

"The notes in the system state that she called you five times last night. The first call was at 9:15 p.m. The second was 10:47 p.m., and the last three were during the eleven o'clock hour. She stated that they all went to voicemail."

Tipping my head to the side, I scratched my chin until the light bulb went off in my head. I was so fucking frustrated after calling Shelly's phone over one hundred times in the morning that I cut my phone off to take my mind off of the bullshit and just focus on Charlie.

"Well, did she leave a message?" I argued.

"It doesn't say so, but I'm not one hundred percent sure, Mr. Fox, as I wasn't here," Ashley stated.

"Alright, whatever. What room is she in?"

"To assure your privacy, she is in the McKeen Pavilion at the Columbia campus. Her room is 904."

"Thanks," I replied before abruptly pressing the end button.

Looking at Shelly as she sat up in the hospital bed inside her private McKeen Pavilion suite disgusted me. Hair disheveled and skin pale and dry, Shelly was almost unrecognizable. She looked worn out and tired, and I had never seen her like that. It wasn't only embarrassing. It was also heartbreaking. While I thought I couldn't hate Shelly anymore after she pulled us into a polyamorous relationship causing more issues than pleasure, my distaste for her was brewing hotter than a mug of warmly toasted coffee, now knowing she was a drug addict.

With arms folded, I stood in front of Shelly's bed as Charlie was by her side, rubbing her head. "How long?" I tersely asked.

Both Charlie and Shelly paused their chit-chat and faced me. Charlie's round eyes were opened wide as a shuddered glow painted her face.

She then slowly shook her head as she gazed directly at me.

Shelly looked utterly confused before opening her mouth. "How long what, baby?" Shelly may not have looked like herself, but she made sure to use her sweet, yielding voice when addressing me. It usually worked, but this time, it repulsed me even more.

Ugh.

"How long have you been a cokehead? And I hope you think really hard before fucking lying to me," I growled, commanding her and Charlie's undivided attention.

Water filled Shelly's reddening eyes as tears came down, which she made no attempt to wipe away. An uncontrollable cry came shortly before she quieted herself by pinching her lips together. She was clearly at a loss for words, but I wasn't having it.

"ANSWER ME!" I shouted.

"I'm not a cokehead, baby."

"Well, according to your toxicology report, you are!"

Tears continued to stream down Shelly's face as her chest caved in and her shoulders dropped.

"Sean, be easy on her. Let's give her the benefit of the doubt and hear what she has to say. It's obvious she needs us right now," Charlie stressed.

I bit my lip hard and raised my hand to my temple as I swallowed a loud gulp. Shaking my head slowly, I contemplated on what to say. I couldn't believe I was looking at the woman I vowed to love for better or worse with so much disdain. There was a time that I thought nothing would cause me to stop loving Shelly. There was a time when I couldn't sleep right if we weren't next to each other, let alone go to sleep if we were bickering. I currently didn't know who she was, and I felt no connection to her. As I stood there stone-faced, I realized that my love was waning, not just because she constantly forced me to break our vows by bringing women into the bedroom, and not because I found out that she was a cokehead. My love was dwindling for Shelly because it was clear I didn't know her, and it was evident she would never be satisfied with me. She would always desire a woman and had no interest in being a mother. And like an epiphany, it blew my mind that I had now realized.

"And all I need to know is how long has she been snorting cocaine?" I stressed, searching Charlie's face defiantly.

Sniffling, Shelly raised her head and shot me a cold look. "If you must know, I haven't had a line of cocaine since 2015 and before then, since college."

My eyes shot open as I exhaled a disappointing breath. "Great, another thing you withheld from me all these years. Who are you really? Because you're not the woman I married, and I can't take any more surprises. This shit is draining, and I have a hospital to run and a baby to prepare for."

"I know, baby, but I'm your wife, and I need you. Think about the vows we made under God. You can't just throw that all away," Shelly pleaded.

"Oh please, don't disrespect my God by using his name in vain to guilt trip me. You're not a believer. You don't go to church. Shit, you don't even pray, so miss me with the bullshit, Shelly. I don't know who the fuck you are, and I don't think I ever have."

Shelly swung her legs off the edge of the hospital bed and hopped off, consequently snatching the IV out of her arm. She jolted past Charlie and leaped forward, forcefully wrapping her arms around me. "Baby, it's me, your wife. The woman you love and the woman that loves you."

Out of the corner of my eye, I saw Charlie cringing as she watched on, pity searing all over her face. Avoiding eye contact with Shelly, and trying to push her off me, she grabbed me by the face, forcing me to look at me. "Baby, I need you," she pleaded.

It took everything in me to push her away because my heart was telling me to stay there and console my wife, but my mind was telling me that she had stopped being mine a long time ago. It just took me longer to figure it out, but now that I knew the truth, I was able to pry her hands off me and turn away, leaving with something that money or love couldn't buy, and that was my dignity.

11
SCANDAL
CHARLIE

CONSIDERING SHELLY WAS STILL IN THE HOSPITAL and would be out of work for at least another week, I cut my leave of absence short. I had a few more weeks left, but now with her gone, I couldn't just leave my staff to feign for themselves. And besides, I had to head back to work to manage any potential damage control due to Shelly's overdose. I wasn't exactly sure what information had gotten leaked, and I needed to get ahead of it.

Feeling like a new woman mentally but adjusting to my pregnant body and all that came with it, such as damning fatigue and mild morning sickness, I strolled to my unit, head high with an ambitious attitude. Being pregnant inspired me to do a little extra than usual, so I adorned my face with a natural beat and spruced up my work outfits. I was sporting a new set of scrubs and bedazzled Crocs, and I even went and got my hair washed and curled.

This time around, being pregnant and making good money would allow me to fully enjoy this pregnancy, and that's precisely what I planned to do. And there was a lot of truth in looking good and feeling good.

Holding my head high, I stepped inside my office and flicked on the lights. It had been a little over two months, so I adjusted my vision to what was in front of me. I dropped my purse and lunch bag onto the sofa, approached my desk, and booted up my computer. Snuggling into my chair reminded me of all the work I had to do, from reviewing the departmental budgets to setting up meetings with my doctors and nurses and preparing for my staff evaluations. It was a little after six a.m. before any of my direct staff was set to arrive, so I had a little less than two hours to get caught up.

As I settled into my computer and pulled up my calendar and database, hoping that work would take my mind off Shelly and Sean, I was highly mistaken. Thoughts of the drama I was now inserted into wouldn't leave my mind. When I first took up the Fox's offer to be their girlfriend, I had no idea it would tear them apart. The way Sean just turned his back on Shelly was heartbreaking to watch but not nearly as painful as Shelly bawling into my bosom as I held and consoled her. I didn't know what to say, so I gently rubbed her back and stayed in the hospital until visiting hours were over. I ordered her food, and we ate and watched TV until she fell asleep. She didn't talk much, which was fine, as the silence between us was refreshing. I knew my presence was more valuable than any advice I could offer. Just like Sean, Shelly needed me to be there, so I was.

After leaving, I returned to Sean and Shelly's condo and buried myself in the bedroom. Jaden was set to graduate in one month, and I had some things to situate for him, so I spent most of the night web surfing, looking up cars, computers, and other tech equipment. Just as I was about to put the laptop away, Sean appeared and snuggled next to me.

"What are you doing?" he asked.

"Just shopping for Jaden's graduation gifts. I want to set up a computer lab in the apartment for him, and I want to get him a car. Something functional, that's not going to bring too much attention," I explained.

Sean picked up my hand and kissed it. "Makes sense. What are you thinking? Nissan? Honda?"

The warmth of his lips comforted me. "Yeah, something like that," I cooed.

"Those are good choices, but I'd personally go with a Kia. They're more masculine than Nissans and better looking than Hondas, and the newest ones have a luxury feel for half the price of a Benz."

"Hmm," I contemplated as Sean grabbed the laptop from me and googled Kia. He pulled up the Kia website and searched for SUVs in the search engine.

"See," he said as he scrolled down the screen, which displayed some beautiful SUVs. When he clicked on one, a panoramic view of cherry-colored seats and a sleek interior really impressed me.

"You were right. My baby worked so hard, so he deserves one of these."

"Of course, I was right, and yes, based on how much you praise Jaden, he definitely deserves a brand-new car. I can't wait to meet him."

Just the thought of Sean meeting my son brought a feeling of dismay over me. I didn't want anything to steal Jaden's shine or take away from his accomplishments. Still, there would be no way to hide the elephant in the room, especially considering that I'd be showing by the time of his graduation. I'd definitely have to explain myself and introduce him to Sean and Shelly and our new addition to the family. I let out an exasperated breath and rested my head on Sean.

As much as I wanted to pick Sean's brain about how he was feeling after leaving the hospital and as much as I felt him wanting to pry more about Jaden, instead, we laid quietly until the sexual urge crept up both of us, causing my coochie to jump and him to slide up in me while kissing my neck. There was something magnetic that pulled us together, making it abundantly clear, without saying a word, that we needed each other.

We made sweet love for the rest of the night, and I orgasmed at least twice. Looking into each other's eyes and kissing softly and slowly, pausing while he was deep inside of me to caress my body was healing to my soul. While I knew I was broken and needed counseling to heal from all the trauma I had experienced from my past and, most recently, Rodney, it felt good to be with Sean, a protector and a provider. He took my mind off the pain, and now knowing that I would be a mother gave me a new sense of purpose. I didn't have time to weep. I had a life to live.

Shaking my head to relieve my mind out of the gutter and focus back on work, as I sat up in my chair, I felt my pussy lips glide together. That always happened whenever I got a Brazilian wax. It also didn't help that I was fantasizing about my sexcapade with Sean last night. Pregnant and horny as fuck, I unraveled the drawstring to my pants and slid my hands to my center. Gently, I parted through the wetness and repeatedly rubbed my clit until uncontrollable moans escaped my mouth. Closing my eyes, I dreamed of Sean and me again, causing me to slide back in my chair, force my legs as open as I could without taking off my pants, and set my feet on my desk. Longing for him, I inserted two of my fingers into my hole and slid them in and out, as I used my other hand to play with my nipples.

Entirely focused on chasing a self-inflicted orgasm, I kept my eyes closed and continued pleasuring myself. Just as I was about to explode, a knock on the door startled me. Without waiting for an answer, the door creaked open, and in walked Sean dressed in a navy blue five-piece suit with a blue and white checkered tie. His eyes immediately bulged open as he caught me pussy handed. Without saying a word, he jolted to my side, pulling me up from the chair and devouring me with intense kisses, which made my leaking pussy throb even more.

We kissed intensely for the next few minutes, causing me to beg for it. "Please, baby, give it to me. I'm going crazy here," I panted between him swallowing my lips.

He blew a chuckle into my mouth as his hands traveled my body. He knew just what to do to make me want more and more. Motioning me toward the sofa, Sean pulled at my scrub top until he pulled it over my head, exposing my bra. Gently, he laid me down and gnawed at my neck, down to my cleavage, as he bit my bra off. My breasts were now exposed, and Sean lapped my nipples into his mouth before circling his tongue around my areola. The wet, warmness from his mouth made me hot as lust traveled through my body. Inching down, his lips trailed south, smooching every crevice of my belly and pelvis until his face met with my throbbing clit. He swallowed me whole, centering his pulsating tongue on my nectar, and sucked it in and out, balancing the pressure with the speed, causing my body to contort. As he sucked and sucked, he grabbed hold of my right foot and massaged it carefully.

"Baby, stop. You're going to make me cum," I cooed, my voice soft and faint as if I was dipping in and out of consciousness.

My moans must have turned him on because he inserted two fingers into my pussy and finger fucked me as he slurped and slurped my pussy in a consistent motion. My legs started shaking, and I started twitching. Just as I was about to cum, the doorknob turned, and a loud gasp imparted.

Karla, my ambitious LPN from Clara Barton High School's nursing program, stood in the doorway with her mouth wide open. Sean jumped up from the sofa, wiped his mouth, and faced Karla, who stood flabbergasted like a child catching their parents having sex for the first time.

"Come inside and close the door behind you!"

"Karla, is it?" Sean pried as I, full of embarrassment, motioned over to pick up my shirt.

"Yes, " she timidly answered.

"My name is Sean Fox. Although I may not know you, I'm sure

you're familiar with me."

"Yes, that's right, Mr. Fox."

"How long have you been working here, and what is your annual salary?"

Karla cleared her throat and rubbed her hands together, giving the impression that she was nervous. "I've only been here for ten months. I'm nineteen years old and a part of the Presbyterian Fellowship. I transferred in from Clara Barton High School seven months ago, so my stipend is currently fifty-thousand dollars a year, subject to increase once I complete the fellowship next September and pass my RN board exams."

Sean lifted his head and scratched his chin. "Well, consider this an early promotion. Your salary will immediately rise to seventy-five thousand dollars, and for the next three months, you will be trained individually by two RNs, a seasoned one and a rookie who just passed the NCLEX, to prepare you to take your state boards in August. Do you think you can handle this level of commitment?" Sean asked, staring Karla into intimidation.

Karla faced him and nodded her head. "Yes, I'm prepared," she sincerely obliged.

Sean smirked and extended his hand to Karla. Karla's eyes traveled up his suit jacket and to his face as she slowly grabbed and shook his hand.

"Thank you. Nurse Thompson will give you five thousand dollars cash at the end of your shift, upon your signing of a non-disclosure agreement and your new employment contract. Starting the next pay period, your salary will reflect your raise, and your individualized training will begin," Sean asserted.

Karla's eyes lit up and her cheeks filled out as she nodded her head in agreement. "Thank you so much, Mr. Fox. You have my complete confidence," she avowed.

"Good. Sit tight here with Nurse Thompson. Your new employment contract, NDA and your five thousand dollars will be on Nurse Thompson's desk in less an hour," he declared, before snatching me up and planting a long, warm kiss on my lips.

"Don't let her out of your sight. I'll email you the documents, print them, and make sure she signs," he asserted.

Mesmerized, I bit my bottom lip and smirked. "Of course, babe."

12
PRESSED
SEAN

"**G**OOD AFTERNOON, MY NAME IS KRISTEN WEAVER," the Senior Vice President and Chief Marketing and Communications Officer here at New York Presbyterian Hospital. We're delighted to be here to update you on some very important departmental changes. I'd like to introduce you to our distinguished leader who has a longstanding legacy with this hospital. Let's welcome our Managing Chief Executive Officer, Mr. Desean Fox."

With a plastered smile on my face, I nodded my head, acknowledging Kristen as she stepped down from the podium and allowed me to take my rightful position on stage. The large conference room we stood in was full of every staff member in the building as the LED brim drop lights dawned on their faces. Swirls of vanilla, caramel, and brown faces, blonde, and chestnut hair, and black and burgundy hijabs stared back at me, reminding me how much of a melting pot New York City really was.

"Hello, everyone. Before we began and get into the meat and bones as to why I called this meeting, I would like to thank you all for your hard work as we welcomed The Koch Foundation partnership a few months ago. There is an enormous amount of work to be done, and we haven't even touched the surface, but I am happy that my team is prepared. After meeting with all the department leaders, I couldn't be more confident," I explained, pausing to smile and chuckle lightheartedly.

To calm my nerves, I focused on Charlie who sat front row and center. Her soft simper sent a soothing feeling through my veins. Shelly used to have that same effect on me. Tipping my head back up and narrowing in on the crowd again, I prepared myself to reveal why I called this meeting.

"Many of you may not know, but my wife Shenelle Fox, our very own Chief Nursing Officer, is experiencing complications with a serious form of ovarian cancer. She is currently receiving treatment and will be out on a leave of absence for some time," I announced and then was shortly bombarded with sighs, grunts, and moans from the audience. "We are currently not sure how long, but in the interim, Nurse Charlestina Thompson will assume the position as CNO and split the nursing director duties between three of our best registered nurses in the hospital," I continued. "Now, at this time. I would like to usher in Nurse Thompson for a few words," I concluded.

Like a deer in headlights, Charlie slowly exited her seat and strolled toward the stage. As she approached the podium, I slid out of her way.

"H-hi, everyone," Charlie stuttered. "I am Charlestina Thompson, director of nursing, now the CNO. I have been at Presbyterian for seven years, having worked my way up from an LPN to an RN, then the head nurse, and two years ago, I was appointed as the official director of nurs-ing. While I am not happy that Shelly Fox, my dear friend, boss, and mentor, will be out for some time, I am up to the challenge of filling her shoes in the interim. I can be found on the eighth floor and am certainly open for any meet and greets, but please do schedule them, as my calen-dar will be booked with duties accompanying my new role." Gracefully nervous, Charlie winced, pinching her lips together, as she nodded twice before saying, "Thank you," and stepping away.

Shortly after. I approached again and centered the attached mic in front of my mouth. "Thank you, everyone. Have a wonderful day!"

"Cheers to your promotion!" I congratulated Charlie as I raised my champagne flute, pushing it forward to clank hers.

"And my substantial raise! Wow, from ninety-five thousand before overtime and one hundred and twenty with it to a whopping two hun-dred and forty-seven thousand dollars a year. I can't believe this. It's almost surreal!" Charlie praised before gulping down the mocktail in her glass.

Seated across from me in front of a candle-lit dinner, on the balcony of our condo, Charlie looked exceptionally beautiful and relaxed. Her skin was glowing against the moonlight. Pregnancy looked so good on her. Considering that the balcony had impeccable lighting that was in-stalled when we first purchased, although it was dark, I could see every shrill and crevice on Charlie's face, from how cheeky her smile was, how her nose was widening across her face and how her lips even were juicer.

"But it's not surreal, baby. This is really our life. I know it may have caught you off guard, but I made the best decision for the hospital, our careers, and our reputation, including Shelly's," I explained, looking down at the crispy Bangkok shrimp the chef prepared as our appetizer.

"I get that, but ovarian cancer? Where did that come from?" she questioned before chuckling and raising her brows at me.

I shrugged and shook my head. "I don't know, it just makes sense. When I think about the fact that Shelly has never gotten pregnant by me, and she only gets her period once or twice a year, it logically makes sense. Besides, as fucked up as it may have been to assign that diagnosis to her, it was better than telling the truth."

Twisting her lip, Charlie pouted. "And how are you so sure that the truth won't get out?"

"Because her records have been permanently deleted from the database and the only copy of her chart is safe with me," I explained.

A sly grin painted Charlie's mouth. "Mr. CEO is always ahead of everything," she noted as she leaned forward and kissed me.

Grabbing her face and not letting go, our tongues swirled around the inside of each other's lips until we decided to take a rest. "Yes, I am, and with you by my side, I'm certain we can hold things down at the hospital until if and when I decide Shelly is cleared to return to work!"

"Whatever you say, Sean. I trust you."

Charlie's words assured me she was up for my leadership, and that turned me on more than I expected. Nonetheless, instead of my bulge stiffening, my heart stirred, and I just wanted to be close to her. "Good, because I trust you too," I responded before turning around and yelling aloud. "Alexa, play 'Slow Jams' by Monica and Usher."

"Dance with me," I asserted, as I stood up from my seat and held my hand out.

As Usher's voice crooned through the speakers, Charlie blushed, lowering her sparkling eyes. She grabbed my hand, and I gently motioned her out of her seat and to the middle of the balcony. Embracing her, we danced slowly under the moonlight for songs on end. There was something about how she touched me, the sweet angelic smell of her perfume that made me feel all fuzzy inside like a little boy, and how connected I felt to her as I rubbed against her growing belly. During these past few weeks, I had been comparing Charlie and Shelly just to cope with my festering anger, but right here in this moment, I knew what I was feeling with Charlie was real.

We continued to dance, and dance, as we shielded each other from the cool late night April breeze. Warming each other with our body heat, we lost track of the songs as a playlist of classic 90s R&B buzzed through the speakers. If I thought for any second that I was the only one feeling our magnetic chemistry, I was proven wrong, when Charlie looked up at me with a face so soft and a voice so sweet and whispered the words "I love you, Mr. Fox."

"I love you too," I expressed as we kissed softly and slowly until I turned her around, nuzzling from the back and rubbing my hands on her belly.

Charlie and I were starting a family.

13
CHANGE OF HEART
SHELLY

"**M**RS. FOX, ARE YOU CERTAIN YUH WANT TUH leave? Mi tink you could benefit from an extra day's stay. We need tuh mek sure you're perfectly hydrated and that your vitals are consistent fuh a few more days to come," the nurse encouraged. I wasn't sure if she was Jamaican or Trinidadian, but her accent was definitely one of Caribbean descent.

"Yes, I'm positive that it's time for me to go. I have a hospital to run," I asserted, looking sternly at the nurse.

It had been two weeks, and I was feeling back to normal. I couldn't spend any more time in there, not knowing what the fuck Sean or Charlie was up to. I hadn't seen Sean since we had the huge fight. He did, however, leave messages with the nurses and sent me flowers once, but I hadn't spoken to him, and he hadn't made an attempt to come and see me. Charlie, on the other hand, visited a few days ago, and being that she's pregnant, I didn't want to bog her down with my issues. She was carrying life, and I knew that was enough to deal with, so I didn't speak about Sean. I just focused on her and her well-being while she inquired about mine. The empathy we shared for each other and how we wore our care on our sleeves was something a man could never understand and one of the reasons I loved women so much.

Sean was just incapable of certain things because he was a man. Considering his silence, the flowers and the calls to inquire about my well-being seemed impersonal. I knew Sean was pissed and most likely embarrassed to find out I had overdosed, but I never expected him to turn his back on me, especially when I needed him most.

Tilting her head forward, the nurse poked her lips out, signifying that I was bullshitting.

"Seriously, I'm fine. As you know, I'm the CNO of this hospital, and I work out of the main building downtown on 68th Street. I have to get home, clean up, and immediately head into the office. I'm sure I have tons of piled-up work waiting for me," I declared as I patted down my blouse, hoping to press out the wrinkles.

The laundry services may have done a decent job of washing the last outfit I was in before my overdose but considering that all my clothes went to the dry cleaners, my shirt and pants were a little too wrinkled for my liking.

The nurse huffed and puffed as she shook her head at least four times. Looking me up and down with a disbelieving qualm on her face, she said, "Whatever you say, Mrs. Fox. Whatever you say."

Her disposition was starting to piss me the fuck off, but I figured it was wiser to reserve my attitude for Sean's ass when I saw him. I grabbed my purse, which contained my wallet, house keys, and my dead phone, and no charger in sight. Then I scurried toward the door. I'd just have to hail a yellow cab to make it home but seeing that the clock read a quarter after seven a.m., I had enough time to make it home, shower, and get to work by ten o'clock at the latest.

It felt so good to take a shower in my home. As nice as the McKeen Pavilion was for a hospital, its shower had nothing on my Grecian marble tiles, waterfall sprout faucet, and scorching hot water. After getting dressed, doing my makeup, and sprucing up my hair to the best of my ability, despite noticing that I was due for a new color application, I met Izzy downstairs in front of my condo.

"Thanks for holding my car down," I stated, looking into her boxy Versace sunglass frames.

She stepped out of the car and walked toward me until we were face-to-face. Dressed in light-colored jeans, an oversized white tee, and a black leather jacket, Izzy was too damn cool for school.

"That's the least I could do after you clunked out on me. How are you feeling?"

"Better than ever. Back to normal," I answered.

Izzy sucked her teeth. "Yeah right. Nobody's back to normal after an overdose, especially someone who doesn't regularly do coke. Trust me when I tell you, stay away from the sugar booger, hunny. It's not for you. You can't handle it!"

"Will you believe this shit? Says the woman who peer pressured me into doing several lines."

Izzy chuckled and held her hands up. "I ain't know your ass was a lightweight. The Shelly I remembered loved to indulge in some good ole fashioned cocaine." Izzy always had to make light of some serious shit.

"Yeah, well, apparently, my body can't handle it anymore."

Izzy steadily nodded her head. "Agreed. Not your thing, and that's okay. I'm really sorry I had to leave you in the hospital. The last thing I wanted was to create any more waves for you and Sean," Izzy sympathetically expressed.

Grabbing her hand, I shook it firmly. "Definitely not the coldhearted, selfish Isabelle I remember. Wow, you're growing."

A calming stare danced across Izzy's eyes. "We're growing," she corrected me. "Take care of yourself, Shelly," she reiterated as she let go of my hand. Before walking away completely, she turned around, and a big Kool-Aid smile appeared, one of her sexiest traits. "And don't ever fucking call me again. Got it?" she stated as she winked.

"Got it!" I affirmed and watched her walk off down the block and disappear in between ongoing jam-packed traffic.

About half an hour later, I arrived at the hospital's main building. It was a quarter to ten o'clock, as expected. I took a deep breath, not knowing what was awaiting me. I wasn't sure if my overdose had gotten leaked. Nonetheless, my nerves settled as I stepped into the building, and my key pass still worked. Security greeted me as usual, which reassured me that all was well. There was no way that Sean would allow that kind of information to get out, for it would undoubtedly ruin his reputation, and Sean wouldn't stand for that. Tapping the balls of my Miu Miu heels on the elevator pavement, my nerves started to rattle again. My palms were sweating as if I was heading into an interview with an unknown employer, begging for a job.

Once off the elevator on the eighth floor, I turned my poker face on and sashayed through the unit. "Good morning!" I greeted them as I looked around at my RNs, who were busy pacing back and forth.

Yvonne, one of my favorite RNs who worked closely with Charlie, jumped back as soon as she saw me. Startled, she did a double take and squinched her eyes. "Good morning. Back so soon. What are you doing here?"

Her question had me on edge. *Did she know? Did word travel that fast?*

The smartest thing for me to do was to play it cool, so I did. I winked at her and said, "It's time to get back to work, baby. This hospital can't run itself, and as well put together my husband is, he can't do this shit without me," I playfully asserted.

"Ahh, sookie now, that's the Shelly I know. She's back!" Yvonne declared, gassing me up.

"You're damn right!" I responded. "Meet me in my office around three for our one-on-one."

"Okay, sure thing. I'll buzz Charlie and the committee in as well."

"Committee?" I asked, puzzled.

"Yeah, the three RNs, that took her position. They report directly to Charlie and me."

Sticking my neck out and squinching my brows, I sniffled. "Excuse me?"

Yvonne retreated, stepping back, and covering her mouth as if she let the cat out of the bag. "Oh, so you don't know?"

"Know what?"

"Nothing I have the authority to enforce, but definitely have a conversation with Charlie, but most importantly, your husband."

I was utterly confused and never felt as undermined as I had since I assumed the position of the CNO. Without saying a word, I nodded to acknowledge that I heard her and stormed off toward Charlie's office. Without knocking, I entered Charlie's office, and from the ghost-like shock on her face, I knew something was up.

"Charlie! What the fuck is going on? Why has a committee assumed your position?"

Fidgeting, Charlie stood up and walked from behind her desk. With a shuddered breath, she exhaled slowly. "Sean held a press conference last week and appointed me to your position as the CNO. As far as my position, we have a managing committee that reports to Yvonne and me while they undergo training."

My temples tensed up as I strained every vein in my face. I was in complete disbelief. "HE DID WHAT?" I roared, my voice shaking the room with terror so strong, even I felt it. Not waiting for an answer, I bit my bottom lip hard until a metal taste peppered my tongue, signaling that I had swallowed blood. "GET SEAN IN HERE NOW!"

Without hesitation, Charlie did as she was told, and within ten minutes, Sean's conniving ass came waltzing through the door.

"Shelly, what's going on? You weren't set to be discharged until next week."

With nostrils inflamed, I couldn't even look at him. With tears in my eyes clouding my vision, I shook my head. "I was in the hospital for two weeks, and you gave my position away?" I asked, heartbroken, on the verge of shaking. "How could you?" I probed before rushing him belligerently and pounding at his chest.

Sean grabbed my hands so quickly as Charlie moseyed herself in the middle of us.

"STOP!" Charlie bickered.

Covering me in a hug to stop me from hitting Sean, Charlie looked me in the eyes. "Relax, Shelly, please. Let's talk about this sensibly," she pleaded.

"See, you're in no shape to even be at work! You're not well, and you have some emotional issues to work out. You need to see a therapist," Sean asserted in a stern tone as if his word was the gospel.

"FUCK YOU!" I yelled.

"You don't mean that. Just like you didn't mean to take a line of coke, or two, or six until you overdosed, huh?" Sean shot back, hitting way below the belt.

At that moment, I couldn't take it, so I jolted past Charlie, elbowing her in the side and rushing Sean again, wailing on him uncontrollably. To protect himself, he held his arms up, blocking my blows until he forcefully grabbed me and threw me across the room. My head hit the wall as I watched my husband run to Charlie's aid.

"Are you okay, baby?" he asked, his voice full of concern.

"Baby?" I questioned loudly with disdain.

He cared about Charlie more than he cared about me.

"Yes, baby, as in my woman who's carrying my baby," he corrected me.

Puzzled, I shook my head and swallowed hard before speaking. "But just a month ago, you kicked her out and wanted nothing to do with her."

With a down-turned mouth, Sean waved dismissively. "Well, my heart has changed for Charlie and for you."

Shifting my gaze between Charlie and Sean, who were snuggled in an embrace, I cocked my head to the side as my forearm muscles started to twitch. "But I'm your heart. I'm your wife. What happened to us?" I pleaded.

Sean inhaled deeply, flexed his fingers, and drew them into fists. "You happened to us, your lust, your dissatisfaction, and your secrets and lies. That's what happened to us, Shelly. You happened to us."

14
NOBODY WINS WHEN THE FAMILY FEUDS
CHARLIE

THE TENSION IN THE AIR WAS THICK BACK AT THE OF-fice for the rest of the day. I so badly wanted to return to my apartment, but I couldn't risk running into Rodney. I was just starting to forget about him since the calls had stopped, and the pop-ups had waned, despite the fact that the detectives still hadn't gotten back to me about the status of his arrest. Being enthralled with Sean and Shelly's drama and the fact that my belly was growing every day was enough to keep me busy. After Shelly came and shook up the room at the office, I tried my best to finish my shift with a clear mind. Boy, was that difficult. I even stayed late at the office to ensure I didn't run into Karla, Yvonne, or any of my immediate staff who may have heard the commotion be-tween us.

Exhausted, I made my way to the condo, and as soon as I entered my key into the lock, Mary J Blige's "Be Happy" bumped through the room. The sweet melody instantly filled my body with a rich joy. The house smelled clean with a mix of heady eucalyptus that put me in a relaxing mood. Although no one was in sight, something told me this was all Shelly.

"Hey!" I shouted through the living room as I made my way inside.

The lights were dim, and as I got closer to the kitchen, the aroma of Latin food hit my nostrils. Cilantro and sofrito floated through the air, meeting me before Shelly's flamboyance.

"Welcome home!" she exulted with a vibrance, a complete one-eighty-degree turnaround from just a few hours ago.

My suspicion arose as I squinched my eyes and glanced at her body up and down. In just a few hours, Shelly had a complete makeover. She transformed her chocolate tresses into a fiery auburn, mirroring her natural red hair. It wasn't only the color, though. It was cut into a layered bob that gave her an edgy sex appeal. Her nails were cut, and her French manicure was freshly done. She was wearing a suggestive two-piece velour sweatsuit. The bottoms were tight shorts that had her ass sitting so right.

"It smells good in here, and you look great, Shellz," I complimented her.

"Thanks, baby," she responded and switched over to me and planted a sensual kiss on my hungry lips.

Shelly sure knew how to put some extra oomph in it as she pursed her plump lips onto mine. She extended the kiss, making sure to leave soft pecks over and over again. The constant tap and savior motion brought extra attention to her mouth. When she finally let go, I noticed her lips were poutier and juicer than I had last remembered.

"Shelly, you went and got some lip fillers?"

"Why, you like?" she shrilled.

Moving closer to her, I analyzed her lips for a second. "Yeah, they feel nice."

"I'm glad you like it, but I didn't get lip fillers. I'm using a hydra-plump lip serum — instant results and no foreign chemicals. I was thinking of lip fillers, but I'm scared. I have seen bad reactions that take a while to heal," she explained. "But the serum was only sixty-nine bucks. Lip fillers are way more costly."

"Good choice. What's for dinner and where's Sean?" I inquired.

Shelly waltzed over to the stove and uncovered two pots. "Dominican cuisine tonight. Classic La Bandera. Stew chicken, white rice, red bean stew, and tostones. I'm about to cut up some lettuce, tomatoes, cucumbers, and avocados for my fresh ensalada," Shelly proudly recited. "And Sean is downstairs in the gym."

"Nice, smells good. I didn't know you could make Dominican food."

Shelly smirked and winked her eye simultaneously.

"Girl, my great-grandmother was Dominican, and my great-grandfather was Haitian, and although my mother raised us in an American household, I grew up in Spanish Harlem. It's not on me, boo. It's in me."

Impressed, I smiled. "Wow, I had no idea."

"Yeah, just remember you don't know everything about me," Shelly slyly stated.

All I could think about was the fact that obviously Sean didn't know everything about her either, but I quieted my thoughts, and smized instead.

"I'm heading to shower and get ready for dinner. This baby has got me ready to eat a cow." I laughed.

"Well, it's more than enough food for you two. Dinner will be ready shortly."

Just as I was about to pick up my laptop bag, Sean's piquant odor met me before I saw his face. Once in my clear vision, I could see that he was sweaty and smelly but nonetheless sexy as hell. Masculinity dripped from his pores and at the sight of him, I just wanted to jump his bones.

"Hey ladies," he greeted us.

"Hey baby," we both responded in unison.

"I'm about to shower and get this sweat off of me. When I'm done, we need to talk," he sternly asserted as he motioned toward the stove where Shelly stood. "Smells good," he complimented her.

Shelly smiled and stuck a spoon in the pot of beans, then raised it to Sean's mouth. He opened wide and devoured it. He chewed several times before swallowing. A bright beam crept up his face as he nodded his head. "It's perfect," he praised.

Shelly's face lit up as she watched him intently. To my surprise, he leaned forward and pecked her on the lips.

"I'm still pissed at you, but them beans are good as fuck. I can't lie," Sean said to Shelly.

Shelly laughed and sucked her teeth. "That's a start."

A few minutes later, after I left the kitchen, I headed to my guest room. I usually showered in Sean and Shelly's bathroom, but seeing as Sean mentioned taking a shower, I wanted to give him his privacy. Undressing, I threw my clothes in the hamper and entered the bathroom. Just as I started to run the shower, I heard the bedroom door open. From the heavy thuds, I knew it had to be Sean. As he slid into the bathroom, his naked body was still beaded with sweat.

He seduced me with his eyes and the churning of his tongue around his lips. From the way he licked them several times in less than a minute, his nickname should be LL Cool J. Without saying a word, he approached me. There was a travel of intensity from his eyes to my body, which commanded me to step into the shower. He followed. Still silent, he grabbed the long-handled loofah and soaped it up. Scrubbing his back with one hand, he grabbed the other handheld loofah, soaped it up with the other hand, and ran it against my back. He then placed both long-handed loofahs down and massaged my back and shoulders softly. I closed my eyes and allowed his hands to travel up and down my spine. When he got to my lower back, he caressed it softly, giving me a relief that I didn't know I needed.

A moan escaped my mouth, and a tingle went down my spine as Sean nibbled on my neck. The water wasn't hitting us at all, instead it created a steam that clouded the shower, and the entire room, I assumed.

"I just want you to enjoy your pregnancy and be at ease, Charlie. I'm sorry for today's commotion. You don't deserve to be pulled into the middle of our drama," he whispered, yet his husky voice held so much intensity as if he were the pope himself.

I turned around and faced him. "It's okay baby, I understand. I'm just grateful to have both of you, good or bad. Every day can't be a holiday." I smirked.

Sean smiled back and leaned down, kissing me quickly. As the water rained down on my back, soothing me into oblivion, I rested my head on his chest, letting out a slow breath. Even in the midst of the drama, both Shelly and Sean somehow expressed their love in an unselfish and unrestrained way. Whew, was I blessed?

"Listen up, ladies! What happened today at the hospital, can never happen again!" Sean warned, staring us both down as his focus shifted from me and then to Shelly.

I swallowed a swig of water and placed my glass back down on the coaster that sat next to my devoured plate of food. At least Sean waited until we finished eating to lay the law down.

"Here's the situation! Charlie has assumed the CNO position momentarily, not indefinitely," Sean explained, looking directly at Shelly, whose lips were pursed as she hung on, eagerly awaiting more information.

"In the meantime, Shelly, I'm ordering you to rehab. You must complete three full months of rehab before you're able to return to the hospital under the condition that you must continue rehab for a full year. And Charlie, I'm ordering you to therapy indefinitely. Now that you're carrying our baby, I want you to be in the best state mentally and emotionally. Understood?" Sean sternly asked, practically demanding an answer from us. Shelly nodded her head several times in agreement, and so did I.

"Good," Sean responded.

"Shelly, just for your information, during the press conference, I announced that you have an aggressive form of ovarian cancer and will be undergoing treatment. That's the story we are sticking to."

Shelly's eyebrows rose. "Ovarian cancer? Now why would you put that on me? Words are powerful."

Sean pushed back in his seat and folded his arms. "Well, we don't have any kids, and we've never been pregnant, so the story adds up. Do you have a better idea?" he scolded her.

Shelly remained mute, her body posture rigid, mirroring her silence.

"Exactly. Anyway, I found the perfect anonymous rehab that's located in the same building and on the same floor as one of the leading oncologists in the city. Again, a perfect cover."

Crossing her arms across her chest, Shelly huffed. "Looks like you've got everything mapped out."

"As the leader of this family, that's my job. We can't afford to be caught slacking. I've worked too hard. Both of you have worked too hard."

I nodded and sipped my water again.

"Now that we've got that out of the way, speaking of family, there are two more things we need to discuss! First off, Jaden's graduation is in two weeks. Charlie and I spoke about getting him a new car. We're thinking a Kia."

A laugh rolled off Shelly's tongue. "A Kia? For a summa cum laude graduate with three job offers? You can't be serious. Jaden deserves a luxury car!"

"He may deserve one, but he's not getting one. Not with my money."

"Well, I'll buy it!" Shelly insisted.

I turned to her, with my nose facing upward. "It's not even about the money. It's the unnecessary attention that comes with a luxury car. My son is a Black man with dreadlocks who presents like one of these drill rappers when he's not cleaned up. I cannot afford for him to have a target on his back from the police or these niggas in the street."

Shelly rolled her eyes. "Whatever you say, Mommy Dearest." She chuckled.

"Anyway, I sure can't wait to meet Jaden and take him under my wing. We need some more masculine energy to balance out the excess estrogen in this house," Sean joked.

"Well, the good news is that the apartment is all ready for Jaden. The housekeeper and interior designer have cleared out all of my and Rodney's stuff. We're just waiting for the furniture to arrive. We have our first delivery tomorrow."

Shelly picked up her glass and took a swig of mint water. "That's exciting."

"Very. His computer desk, desktop and laptop are on its way as well. The housekeeper will let the furniture folks in, and I've paid Geek Squad to set everything up."

"Perfect because you know I don't want you setting foot in there unless we're with you," Sean asserted.

"Yes, I know," I obliged.

Sean scooted his chair back to the table and grabbed a hold of his beer and swooshed down a swig. "Lastly, it's about time that we start preparing for the arrival of the baby. Have you signed up for Lamaze classes yet, Charlie?"

"Yeah, they start the first week of June," I answered.

"Sounds good. I'm excited," Sean said.

I quickly turned to face Shelly, who's stony face transformed into a fake plastered smile. If I wasn't mistaken, it was becoming clear that Shelly was growing jealous of me and the baby. Every part of me didn't want to believe that she was envious, considering that she initiated this polyamorous relationship and was ecstatic when she found out I was pregnant, but as time went on, situation after situation was showing her deck, that she had a jealous joker card in her hand. And whenever she felt like it, she would throw that bitch on the table. My eyes scanned her face closely, spotting the rising color in her cheeks.

Shelly was threatened by me. The fucking irony.

I turned forward to face Sean and a sneaky grin peppered my mouth, as I said, "Me too."

The rest of the night was full of sexy R&B, rich and decadent delicacies, and mocktails. We drank, laughed and slow danced, all together. Shelly and Sean drank wine, and I had a fruity mocktail with a strong, grenadine that produced a bubbly sensation that had me feeling good. Not intoxicated good, but in the moment good and sexy good. As I stepped back from the circle, allowing Sean and Shelly some alone time, watching them sway against each other's body was turning me on.

I sat back on the couch with my legs crossed, twirling my champagne stem, and rubbing my ankles against my smoothly waxed legs. Touching myself ignited my fire, and watching these two dance and kiss made my nipples harden. I unbuttoned my satin top and then licked my index and middle finger before coating my nipple with warm saliva. Immediately, my center moistened, begging me to slide my fingers inside my entrance. Since I became pregnant, my pussy was extra wet, to the point I had to wear panty liners to catch the excess juice from leaking. I closed my eyes, cocked my legs open and positioned both feet on the couch. My lips had budded, my flower was exposed, and my clit was pulsating. As I flicked it back and forth, I moaned again and again. This pregnancy had me so horny.

In a split second, I felt hands caress my legs and extend it from out of the seated position. I opened my eyes and Shelly was smiling as she swooped down and spat directly on my pussy. She then lapped up the juices in a quick motion, causing my legs to shake. Moment later, Sean appeared and stuffed his dick inside my mouth. As she ate me and he fucked my face, the sensation surged through my body.

Shelly continued licking and licking, then inserted a finger deep inside of me that hit my uterus. She pulsed her middle finger steadily causing me to push Sean's dick out of my mouth and cry out from the overwhelming pleasure. "Oh my god, Shelly! Oh my god!" I screeched.

She kept going and refused to stop until water came shooting out of my pussy. With her mouth open, she caught every juice and twirled her wet tongue around her lips. Shortly after, she got up from the floor, shimmied out of her velour shorts, and bent off on the couch. Holding her ass cheeks open, she turned her head toward Sean, who stood behind the couch, jacking his dick.

"I want it in my ass tonight, baby."

A sexy, yet confused smile danced on his face as he motioned toward us. I watched him shove Shelly's head into the couch and get on his knees. Sticking his tongue out, he licked her from front to back like a baby wipe. Consequently, Shelly giggled like a little kid. Sean then stood up and slapped his meaty wood on her ass. Shelly then spread her ass cheeks further apart and Sean pushed the head of his dick slowly into her ass. It took several inches and grunts to get it inside, but as soon as he did, Shelly's moans overflowed. This was the loudest I ever heard her, and the most beautiful pleasure ridden expression I ever witnessed on her face, although it was plastered by Sean's heavy hand as he delivered smooth strokes in her ass.

While I had never dabbled in anal sex, the way Shelly was enjoying it, made me eager to try it.

Damn, these motherfuckers were some freaks!

15

A BLESSING IN DISGUISE

SHELLY

THINGS WERE SLOWLY RETURNING TO NORMAL AT home despite the three times a week I had to attend rehab. Sean and I weren't fighting. In fact, we were talking more than usual and even discussed attending couples' therapy. Well, it was my idea. Considering that he ordered Charlie to go to therapy, I figured we should attend too, and he agreed. Still, we haven't yet found a therapist who fits both of our needs and preferences, and it would definitely have to wait, seeing as we were on our way to Penn State University to watch Jaden walk across the stage and get his degree.

"We should be to our destination in forty-five minutes," the Spanish driver stated as he adjusted his rearview mirror and looked me directly in the eye.

I nodded my head, acknowledging him, then pulled out my phone to check my email and track my delivery. Everything was right on time. By the time we finished eating at Del Frisco's, my gift to Jaden should be waiting.

Sean, who was seated next to me, said, "Thanks for beating this crazy traffic, boss. You're a great defensive driver."

"No problem, sir," he responded.

I turned around and eyed Charlie who was spread out in the third row.

"You okay, babe?"

Feet up and relaxed, she smiled. "Yup, I'm good. I just can't wait to see my baby walk across that stage."

"I can only imagine how proud you are. Shit, we're proud of you for getting him this far and we're proud for you," I praised Charlie as I looked at her visible baby bump.

It was amazing how quickly she started to show. In the matter of a month, she was big, which made sense, since her doctor just informed us earlier in the week that she was sixteen weeks.

"Thank you, and thanks for doing this with me. You guys haven't even met Jaden but have already taken him in. I just hope all of this isn't too overwhelming for him," she winced, pursing her lips. "The last thing I wanted was for my baby bump and my relationship with y'all to steal his shine, but I know my baby. Things will make sense for him as soon as he meets you all."

"I think so too, and I just want to thank you for allowing Sean and me to be a part of this special day for you," I said, then patted her leg softly.

Crowded in the stadium seats watching the faculty call name after name wasn't as nerve-racking as beating the commotion to find Jaden. Squeezing through traffic as Sean dragged me along, following Charlie caused me to bump into several people and even stumble. With a plastered simper on my face, I apologized every time I knocked against someone. It was truly annoying, but the attendees showed grace and didn't make a big deal out of it.

From behind Sean, who was a few inches taller than me, I focused my gaze from the side and caught a glimpse of Charlie a few inches ahead of us. She stopped in dead traffic as I watched strong arms wrap around her. Once they broke their embrace, I caught a glimpse of Jaden's bewildered expression as his eyes traveled down to Charlie's midsection. A few seconds later, we approached Charlie from the back, and Jaden's jaw locked as he stared us up and down.

Charlie grabbed Jaden by the hand and dragged him out of the ongoing traffic of people to the side near the stadium windows. We followed suit and Jaden's aggressive grimace hadn't waned.

"I want you to meet two very special people. This is Shelly and Sean," Charlie introduced us.

Sean extended his hand forward and Jaden's hazel eyes trickled up Sean's entire arm. Jaden left Sean's hand hanging, so I intervened.

"Hi, I'm Shelly. It's nice to finally meet you. We've heard so much about you." I smiled.

"And who the fuck are you?" Jaden snarled.

"Jaden, watch your mouth. Shelly and Sean are twice your age and older than me. Show my people some fucking respect."

Jaden sucked his teeth. "I'm trying to figure out why you want to introduce me to these folks rather than your baby's father. Since you decide to show up to my graduation with such a big surprise, how about we start there with the obvious? Who are you pregnant by?"

"So, you went from Rodney's bum ass to a poly relationship with a married couple? You can't be serious, ma?" Jaden scoffed. Sitting erect in his seat, he brushed his long dreadlocks from out of his face as his eyes bounced back and forth between the three of us. "And now you're pregnant," he sneered, slowly shaking his head.

We were seated inside of a private party room at Del Frisco's. Thank God we were in a secluded, closed off area because this conversation wasn't for the public to hear.

I sipped on my cocktail, attempting to play coy and not look as interested in the bickering. Instead, I blocked out the noise around me and studied Jaden. He was tall, much taller than Charlie, so his height must have come from his dad. He had the stature of a football player. A strong, meaty neck, broad arms, and a built back. It was obvious he worked out as much as he ate, considering the two large ribeye steaks he ordered.

"Look Jaden, I don't need your judgement. Leaving Rodney wasn't easy, but it was necessary and despite what you may think, I'm very happy. Sean and Shelly are wonderful people and have made these last few months very comfortable for me," Charlie explained.

"I bet!" Jaden shot back and kissed his teeth.

Sean took a deep breath and rested his hand on my lap under the table. "Jaden, I know this may have been a lot for your mother to spring on you, especially during your graduation, but I'll have you know, man to man, that your mother is in good hands. I wanted to meet you to personally let you know that my wife Shelly and I love and care for your mother very much, and that love, of course, is extended to you. We are all so proud of you and all your accomplishments, and we are here to help in any way possible," Sean avowed with an earnest simper on his face.

I nodded my head and smiled immediately after. "Yes, Jaden we are so proud of you. That's why we wanted to give you this gift, as a token of appreciation," I announced.

Jaden's brows raised as he watched me rummage through the bag beside me. A feeling of giddiness came over me as I prepared myself to impress not only him but Charlie and Sean. I just wanted to do something special because it always gave me a boost to give to others. Pulling out a green box, I sat it on the table and slid it toward Jaden.

His eyes widened as he looked down at it. Charlie leaned over the table, her neck protruding out as she squinched her eyes to look at the box.

Jaden flipped it open and shook his head profusely. "Nah," he crowed. "You got me a Rolley?" Jaden's eyes beamed, and a glow instantly appeared on his face.

A scowl crept up Charlie's face as she folded her arms. "Shelly, you got my son a Rolex?"

"Yeah, ma. This shit is fly!" Jaden exclaimed as he placed the diamond, gold Rolex on his right wrist.

"Sean, did you know about this?" Charlie asked, turning directly to Sean who also had a frown on his face.

"No, I didn't," he scoffed.

"Shelly, really? If I didn't want my son to have a luxury car because of the attention that came with it, what makes you think I want him prancing around New York City with a fucking Rolex?" Charlie was fuming, spit flying, and white foam crusted around the corners of her mouth. "Are you trying to get my son killed?"

"No, of course not!" I answered defensively.

"Ma, chill. You already know I ain't gon' be walking or in the hood around no lame ass bums, anyway. All of my college friends from New York come from money. I'm good!"

"Jaden, that's not the fucking point. The point is, I spoke with Shelly and Sean about this type of shit already, and she completely disregarded my requests."

"Come on, ma. Don't trip. It was okay for you to insert these people into my life without warning, but now that they want to do something nice for me it's a problem. You're bugging!" Jaden huffed.

"Watch your mouth when speaking to me. I'm not going to tell you one more fucking time. I don't care how grown you are. I don't care that you graduated and got three fancy job offers, you're going to respect me!" Charlie angrily asserted. The vein in her temple was engorged and nearly protruding out the side of her head. With a tense face, she turned to me.

"Shelly, what you did was out of line. You can return the watch because Jaden's not keeping it!"

Bewilderment written all over his face, Jaden turned to Charlie swiftly. "Nah, ma. I'm not. This is an investment piece. Fuck wearing it. I can auction it off in several years."

"Exactly!" I interjected. "When I bought this for Jaden, I was thinking about the future. My second gift to him is for right now." I snickered. "In fact, I just got word that it has just arrived." I announced as I responded to the text. "Come on, guys. Follow me outside!"

I got up from my seat, and Jaden hopped up immediately. Charlie and Sean both dragged their feet but eventually staggered along. As soon as we stepped out of the restaurant doors, a white Mercedes Benz convertible stood in front of us with a red bow on it.

"Congratulations on graduating summa cum laude, Jaden!" I yelped.

Floored, Jaden's mouth fell open as he circled the car. His hands were covering his mouth as he shook his head. "This all me?"

I nodded happily. "Yes, it's all you! 2021 Mercedes Benz convertible. Used, but practically new with only eight thousand miles on it. Fully paid off so you own it. The insurance is in my name and in a year, when you're situated with work, it will be transferred to you."

Jaden swooped around the car and hugged me tight. "Thank you so much. I can't believe this." Jaden quickly let me go and ran toward his mother who was standing with her hands on her hips. "Do you see this, ma? It's mine!" he yelled as he wrapped his arms around Charlie, who stood stiffly, not embracing him.

It was obvious that Charlie was pissed off, but she reserved her silence. Jaden then released her and approached Sean and dapped him up. "Thank you, man. I appreciate you and your wife!"

Sean nodded his head and tightened his lips together without saying a word.

"You know, this poly relationship don't sound too bad after all. I get a bonus mom and a dad I never had. I guess this is a crazy twisted blessing from God and who am I to question the Father?"

16

GO HARD

JADEN THOMPSON

I PRESSED MY FOOT ON THE GAS AND THAT SHIT SKIRTed off the pavement of the restaurant. A nigga never felt better. I was driving a damn near brand new car, a drop-top Mercedes Benz at that, and I had a bad bitch riding shotgun. Well, excuse my rudeness. Shelly was a lady. She was a divine woman, and it was evident from how she smelled, to her classy French manicured tips, her smooth caramel legs, and that sexy red wavy bob she sported. Everything about her intrigued me. She may have been twenty years older than me, but she made a nigga feel young again, like a little ass boy. Shit, my stomach was fluttering, and I wasn't sure if it was the car or being in the company of the most elegant yet equally gorgeous woman I ever met in my twenty-one years of living.

"You liking your new car, huh?" Shelly chided. I glanced at her quickly and noticed she was adjusting her Chanel shades. They fit her face perfectly.

"Call me Ronald McDonald! I'm loving it!"

Shelly chuckled. "Ain't you a little too young to know about Ronald

McDonald? Does your generation even eat McDonalds anymore?"

"Nah, not really. When I was in elementary and middle school, we did, but now it's either Chick-fil-A or crab legs!" I exclaimed over the beating wind.

"Sounds about right!"

I peered down at my phone to eye the directions as I wasn't familiar with the route from York, Pennsylvania, as I had never driven to the city from school. In a slight second, Shelly snatched the phone out of my hand.

"No texting! I'll direct you. Just drive!" she insisted.

I kissed my teeth so seductively that a smooching sound persisted out. I couldn't help but flirt with her. It was just something about Shelly that made me want to discover everything she was hiding under her shell and why she was married to a square like Sean. I mean, he wasn't a complete square, but he was so polished, and it was evident he hadn't been through shit and knew nothing about struggle.

"Alright, alright, you got it." I smirked. "Well, if you're going to take my phone, at least put some music on."

"Sure. What you want to hear?"

"That new Baby! Put on 'Go Hard'!" I requested.

"Look boy, I don't listen to all that Trap Cap bullshit y'all call music. I come from the Bad Boy, Ruff Ryders era, real music."

"Yeah, yeah, yeah. Well, just think of me as Diddy and you as Caresha sexy ass. You may come from the Bad Boy era, but only a man can show you a real bad boy. Now put that Baby on, like I said!" I forcefully demanded, then squeezed her leg. I knew my move was bold, but I needed to gage her reaction to determine if I was doing too much or just enough.

When Shelly giggled and didn't move her leg away, I knew she was game, and I was about to show her what it was like to fuck with a young lit nigga.

Baby's voice crooned through the speakers, and I cranked that shit all the way up as I revved that gas. The car belted forward, accelerating until I hit one hundred miles an hour. Although my head was straight and my sight was focused on the road, I knew Shelly was anxious from how tightly she gripped my thigh.

"I'm back goin' hard again, I'm shuttin' down my heart again
No one can get next to me, so they gotta put orders in
Try my best to act like I didn't care, but I can't hold it in and
I'm not into losin', I go hard as I can go to win."

When Baby rapped that shit, it hit so much because I was twenty-one years old with a degree in the IT field, three job offers, and a new whip. Shit, life couldn't get any sweeter than this.

Three and a half hours later, we were heading down the Hudson River Greenway from The Bronx into Harlem. I'm not sure which way moms and Sean drove, but they were still an hour out. I guess the fact that I was consistently pushing eighty miles per hour explains why they were still in Upstate New York. The ride with Shelly was smooth. We split half of the time listening to trap and the other half going down memory lane listening to 90s and 2000s R&B. Most of my peers didn't know half of the music that Shelly was playing, but growing up with a mother like mine meant Saturday mornings we cleaned to Mary J Blige, Jodeci and Dru Hill and Sundays we blasted R. Kelly, Patti LaBelle, and Monica.

"Somebody loves you bay bay! Oh, oh, oh!" I belted out, singing along to the famous Patti LaBelle song I requested a few minutes ago.

"What you know about Patti boy?" Shelly asked.

"More than you'd know. I love the original and many of the remakes. Throw that K. Michelle and Trina song on 'If It Ain't Me'. K. Michelle killed that."

A blush of surprise crept up Shelly's face as she chuckled. "I'm surprised you even listen to K. Michelle. How old were you when she was on *Love & Hip Hop*? Wow."

"Don't worry about it!" I baited. "But I watched it, so I'm hip. I'm telling you now, don't sleep on the young boy." I smirked, as I pulled my second spliff from behind my ear and lit it.

I inhaled, took a long pull, and exhaled a thick white fog of smoke. Quickly glancing over at Shelly, her mesmerized eyes danced over me. If I wasn't careful looking at her for too long, I could very well cause an accident. I focused my eyes back on the road before speaking.

"You sure you don't want to hit this?" I asked, offering her the spliff once again and expecting her to also decline.

To my surprise, she grabbed the spliff from me and inhaled deeply, then paused and almost spat up a lung from how much she was coughing.

"Take it easy, little mama. Like Amanda Seales says, small doses."

Shelly coughed a bit more, then laughed. "Wait, you listen to Amanda Seales' podcast too?"

"Not anymore, but I used to a hell of a lot with my ex. She was into it. I can't lie. Amanda be talking about some real shit. These other podcasters don't be talking about nothing!"

"Ain't that the truth!" Shelly agreed.

"Yeah, but I know you ain't that out of touch that you're violating the cardinal role of weed smoking."

Puzzled, Shelly took another pull and shrugged.

"Puff, puff, pass. You over there, chiefing," I joked.

Shelly jumped in her seat and shoved the spliff in my face. "Oh, I'm sorry!" She quickly apologized with a hint of angst.

"You good, ma. I was just joking."

I could hear the anxiety settle from Shelly's chest as she hit me in the arm. It stung but didn't hurt. It actually felt sort of like a love tap.

"Boy, quit playing," she warned.

"Alright, alright. No more playing."

"Good, now turn into here. This is my building," Shelly instructed me to turn into the valet circle of a decked-out condo building across the street from Central Park West.

"Dayummm. You live here?" I fanned out.

"Yeah, don't start acting like a groupie now," Shelly jested.

I sucked my teeth loud and long, mimicking my Jamaican best friend from Penn State. "Oh, please. I don't wanna hype ya, but it takes a lot to impress me," I flirted.

"Oh really? Well, I think I've already done that twice today!" Shelly blustered.

After I put the car in park, I leaned over to her and bit my bottom lip. "Aiight, you got it, but don't rub it in," I snickered.

Shelly chased me with her eyes before reaching for the door. I immediately hopped out. "Nah, I got that."

"Well, actually, Ramon should have, but he looks occupied," she said, pointing in the direction of a Hispanic man whose neck was bent over as he typed away on his cell phone.

"Man, fuck Ramon. I got you!" I insisted as I hopped to open her door.

As Shelly stepped out, one foot in front of the other, so meticulously and dainty-like, I studied every crevice of her body. She was tall, at least six feet, but she wasn't taller than me, thank God. And If I wasn't mistaken, I was a bit taller than Sean, not to mention I was younger, which gave me a slight advantage over her husband. As she twirled around, heading over in Ramon's direction, my mouth slid open, and I was left with the stuck face. She had a thick ass on her and stealthy calves. Now that I got a really good look at her, I knew what I felt was more than a little crush. I was digging Shelly.

"Let me give you a tour and show you where you'll be sleeping," Shelly said as she strutted through her condo. I watched her intently, studying every stride she took. Her posture was straight and erect. Her neck was long as she spoke with so much confidence. She was confident yet warm.

Damn. Mom lucked up with these two!

My thoughts were buzzing as my eyes bounced from wall to wall, marveling over the fancy, expensive art, and décor fixtures. Not only was their crib laced, but it also smelled good.

"This is your room. It started as your mom's guest room, but now she spends most of her time in our room, so I'm sure she won't have a problem with you using it."

I stepped inside, and the bedroom set alone sold me. All I needed was a desktop, laptop, and printer, and I'd be good.

"Yeah, I'm pretty sure she won't."

"Nope. Now, make yourself at home. I'm about to order some food. Do you want anything in particular?" Shelly quizzed, her eyes low and pink.

"Ahh shit. Somebody's got the munchies!"

Shelly's cheeks puffed out, and a sly smirk blushed on her face. "Yeah, a little."

"Well, you're the one that's hungry, so order whatever you want."

Shelly rubbed her hands together like an excited toddler. "I'm in the mood for some Italian." She flicked her wrist to view the time on her Apple Watch. "Carmines is still open! I will order a few things for your mom and Sean, too. Do you like Lasagna? Calamari? Alfredo?"

"Yeah, all that shit sounds good," I affirmed as I licked my lips and stepped closer to Shelly, invading her private space.

Just as I was about to do the unthinkable, the persistent sound of footsteps became closer and closer until I heard Sean's voice and my mother's laugh.

17
THE GAZE OF THE SOUL
CHARLIE

AS SOON AS WE ENTERED THE CONDO AND JADEN and Shelly swung around the corner like two giddy school kids, I knew something was up. Shelly's posture and stagger were off. Her shoulders were slumped, and her eyes were red. Jaden, on the other hand, seemed normal except for his googly eyes that couldn't stay off of Shelly. He had a protective air that was all too familiar to me because it was the same way he revered me whenever we were in public. The only difference was that we were inside, and instead of me, he was shielding. It was Shelly. I instantly grew hot as my defenses rose.

"Gather your things, baby boy. I'm taking you to the house. I have a few surprises for you!" I exclaimed joyfully, despite Shelly stealing my shine and trying to outdo me by showering my son with extravagant gifts he didn't need.

Jaden's shoulders rose as he bit his lip. Shaking his head, he stepped closer to Sean and me. "Shelly showed me to my room. She said I can sleep there." Jaden turned around and extended his arms open. "It's lit in here! And besides, I want to spend my first night with you!"

His words warmed my heart, reminding me of when he was an innocent little boy clinging to his momma's leg and crying out whenever I dropped him off for daycare. Damn, I missed those days. At first, I was happy knowing he was becoming a man and my baby-raising days were over, but now carrying a baby myself, I knew I'd have to start again from scratch. It was daunting but exciting the more and more my stomach grew.

"That's sweet baby, and I want to spend the night with you too, but not here. I really have some things I want to show you and talk about with you alone. So, I may stay over with you at the house."

Sean rested his heavy hand on my shoulder. "Nah, baby, that's not a good idea. You know how I feel about you being in that apartment alone."

Jaden's eyebrows raised, and I knew he was confused so I intervened.

"I won't be alone. Jaden will be there with me," I explained.

"I know that, but I just don't feel comfortable with either of you there, considering—" Sean said before being rudely interrupted by Shelly.

"Agreed. I don't feel comfortable with either of you staying there alone, which is why I showed Jaden to the guest room. He knows he's able to occupy it as long as need be."

Shaking my head, I waved my right hand dismissively, warding off Shelly's statement. "Listen, we already spoke about this. Jaden is staying at the apartment because it now belongs to him. He is a young man who is growing. He needs his own space. Besides, he smokes a hell of a lot of weed, and I know y'all ain't with that," I informed him.

"Yeah, that's for sure," Sean stated. "It may be decriminalized in the city, but we are the only Black couple in this building. We don't need that kind of heat."

As Sean spoke from behind me, I couldn't see his expression, but the guilt was written all over Shelly's face and body as she fidgeted, twiddling her thumbs. While I didn't want to burst her bubble, my usual regard for her waned as soon as she overstepped with my son by buying him a Benz and Rolex after I made it clear I didn't want Jaden walking around like a trap rapper or athlete. He was already a target. He was Black, masculine, and he had dreadlocks. I worked hard to keep my son out of the streets and ensure he graduated from college. I wouldn't dare lose him to the streets now.

"Shelly, are you high?" I questioned.

Watching her squirm brought me so much comfort. Sean was repulsed by Shelly's cocaine overdose, that the thought of her doing any drugs, even if it was just weed, would put an even bigger wedge between them two. And since Shelly tried her hardest to get in between me and my son, she was just going to have to lay in the bed she made.

At the sound of my accusation, Sean stepped from behind me and invaded Shelly's space, analyzing every crevice of her face. "Shelly, look at me!" he demanded.

"Sean, relax, damn!" she spat.

"Fuck you mean, relax. Look at me and answer the damn question. Are you high?"

Shelly lifted her head and looked into Sean's eyes, her hand on her hip defensively.

Sean shook his head and sucked his teeth. "You can't be fucking serious. You're in fucking rehab, and you're out here smoking weed. At least coke rids out of your system within twenty-four hours, but THC takes weeks to clear out of the body. I can't believe you, Shelly," Sean fumed before turning away.

From the look on Jaden's face, I could tell he was embarrassed for Shelly as he stepped closer behind her as if he was shielding her.

"Fuck you, Sean! Don't you try to belittle me like I'm some fucking drug addict!" Shelly bickered.

"But you are. It hasn't even been a month of rehab, and here you are, picking up another bad drug habit."

Grabbing ahold of Jaden's arm, I said, "Come on, baby, get your things. We need to give Sean and Shelly some time to cool off."

"I'm cool. I have nothing to say to Shelly," Sean interjected.

"And ma, I told you I want to stay here tonight with you!" Jaden insisted.

"Jaden, no, now I'm not going to repeat myself. Get your things and go."

Shelly stepped forward and grabbed Jaden's other arm. "Charlie, this is my house, and Jaden is more than welcome to stay. You can't make him leave."

"This is my house too, and out of respect for Charlie, I won't insist that Jaden leaves, but we will. Come on, Charlie, let's go," Sean directed as he pulled me away from my son and a woman I once looked up to.

"How could she just overstep and try to outdo me for my own son's graduation?" I vented to Sean as he held me and rubbed my belly. We were lying in bed inside a fancy suite in the Trump Palace a few miles from the condo.

"That's Shelly for you! It's in her nature. Excellence over excuse and at the expense of anybody. She's done the same to me. Before my mom and dad passed, she'd always give them better gifts than me on Christmas. She even tried it with my sister's husband. One year she gave him a Harley Davidson, knowing my sister couldn't afford it. Because she always played nice with my sister, avoiding arguments despite the fact that they didn't get along, she'd use nicety tactics to get under my sister's skin, which explains why my sister and I are estranged," Sean explained.

I was stunned but not at all shocked or surprised, knowing how snooty Shelly really was. It was amazing how you could admire someone, but as soon as you got to know them on a deeper level, admiration could easily turn into disdain.

"Damn, baby. I'm sorry to hear that."

"Yeah, and I'm sorry about everything with Jaden. I figure we would enjoy the night and start over tomorrow. I'll take you and him over to your old apartment so he can get settled, and then I'll leave you two alone, but I'll have security guarding your door and the building for your safety. For you and Jaden's safety."

I smiled, my heart beaming with gratitude. "What did I do to deserve such a caring man like you?"

"Carry my baby," Sean jokingly said.

I elbowed him in the side, and he grabbed me tighter, as he laughed.

"Now, don't start getting handsy with me, now, girl. All jokes aside, Charlie, at first, when Shelly introduced you to our relationship, I wasn't thrilled. As I explained before, I'm a one-woman man. However, when I slid up in you raw that first time, I let my guard down a bit. I was like, with pussy this good, I may have to reconsider this poly shit again," Sean admitted, starry-eyed.

"Yeah, yeah, but what about when you found out I was pregnant and started acting all funny? What was that about?" I asked as I sat up in the plush king-sized bed and poked my lips out. "Yeah, don't think I forgot," I taunted him.

Exhaling a deep breath, Sean turned to me, gazing deeply into my eyes as he grabbed my hand into his. "Charlie, it's no secret that if it weren't for Shelly, we would have never been intimate as we have been. Still, my love for you is building, not only because of the baby but because of your charm, warmth, and how you make me feel. I don't feel like I constantly have to play mental gymnastics when talking to you, as if you have some calculated agenda. You're genuine, and it's a breath of fresh air. Besides, you're fun as fuck. We have so much in common, and you're a woman of God. I know raising our son in the church won't be an issue with you. I never thought I would say this, but I think I'm falling in love with you," Sean confessed.

Stunned, I covered my mouth with my hands. I couldn't believe the words coming out of Sean's heart. This was the same man who, nearly three months ago, kicked me out when he found out I was pregnant. While I believed Sean would be an incredible father, I wasn't too sure he could be the man I gave my heart to fully. Lastly, although I was angry with Shelly, she was still my friend, my mentor, and a woman I admired and grew to love. I couldn't just take her husband away from her. Well, maybe when Sean said he was in love with me, he meant he was in love with me and Shelly. Nonetheless, before deciding, I had to know the real deal.

"And what about Shelly?" I asked concerningly.

Sean shook his head back and forth and shrugged his shoulders. "I've been battling with this for the last few months as I've thought about all Shelly and I have been through. The good and the bad, the ups and the downs. The truth is that I loved Shelly more than she loved me for years, to the point that my excessive love for her forced me to fall out of love with her and in love with you."

I tried my best to make sense of all that I was hearing, but it was incomprehensible. Sensing my confusion, Sean grabbed the sides of my face.

"Shelly's a lesbian, and I've known it for a long time. You're not. Shelly doesn't want kids, and even if she did, she's a pleasant woman, but she doesn't have the mother gene. You do. I can sense it. I can see it in your eyes. You don't want to share me, and you don't want to raise a child with two mothers and one daddy. You don't want the burden or the kind of life that warrants unnecessary drama or attention."

Tears were streaming down my eyes as I took in Sean's words because he was absolutely right. I hadn't been able to process my true feelings surrounding this pregnancy because I was so busy preparing for Jaden to come home. I had to return to work and take over Shelly's position, and then counseling had me revisit a lot of my past, so much so that I couldn't focus on the future, but Sean's words covered everything that subconsciously was in my mind. While I enjoyed the perks of this polyamorous relationship, I just wanted one person, my own man, and my own family. While all the words were forming in my head, I couldn't find it in myself to express them loudly, so instead, I grabbed Sean by the neck and kissed him deeply.

Some things and situations didn't call for words, just appropriate reactions.

18
SPAZZ OUT
RODNEY

"**I**KNOW YOU TOLD ME NEVER TO CALL YOU AGAIN, but I have some valuable information that I'm willing to share if you Zelle me three hundred dollars right now," my PI, who I fired a few weeks ago, shared anxiously through the phone.

"This better be damn fucking good intel," I spat.

"Look at you. Been watching a lot of crime shows lately, huh? Picking up the lingo and whatnot?" he jested, trying to be funny.

"Nigga, fuck you! Just cough up the information."

"Cough up my cash, buddy. My Zelle is waiting."

I rolled my eyes as I scanned the large lunchroom where all the other pitiful Amazon workers scarfed down their food and guzzled their beverages at record speed, hoping to beat the measly fifteen-minute break time.

"All right. Give me a second," I grouched as I pulled up the Chase mobile banking app, logged in, and sent the Zelle payment to his account.

Looking at my account, which had six hundred and ninety dollars left, I shivered. The twenty thousand dollars I came up on after pawning Charlie's jewelry was gone already. I got an apartment in one of those new apartment buildings, paid my rent for a few months, and furnished my crib. Between bills and daily living expenses, I was down to my last thousand dollars before breaking this nigga off with three hundred.

"I just received it. So, look, I just got word from the security guard that I paid off, that Charlie, her son, and the Fox's were spotted entering her apartment building two days ago. The Fox's left shortly after, but Charlie and her son haven't as of yet."

My shoulders rose as my blood boiled with excitement. "Good shit, my guy. I don't get out of work until the morning, and then I have to return right back here in less than twelve hours for my next shift. I won't be able to make it there until the end of the week when I'm off." I rationalized my schedule in my mind.

"Yeah, man, well whatever you do, don't do nothing too crazy and leave the Fox's out of it," the PI warned, pissing me the fuck off.

"What the fuck, nigga? Do you work for them or something? Why are you so worried about me stepping to them?" I spazzed, my voice elevating, causing a few people at the other table to look at me.

"I've already made myself clear when it comes to the Fox's. They are uncharted territory, and I strongly advise against going after them. You don't have the money, the resources, or the network it would take to go toe to toe with Desean Fox."

"SHUT THE FUCK UP!" I screamed. With all my rage, I violently flipped the table standing in front of me over, and my lunch splattered onto the floor. "I'M TIRED OF YOU TELLING ME WHAT I DON'T HAVE. YOU DON'T FUCKING KNOW ME!" I roared into the phone before hanging up.

As I looked up, all eyes were on me, and my area manager was storming toward me with a radio plastered to her mouth.

"Kane, HR right now!"

With my head down, I trotted behind my area manager into the Human Resources office, where I was met by an anorexic-looking African girl with a navy-blue head wrap on her head. While it wasn't a Hijab, from prior run-ins with her, I knew she was Muslim.

The Human Resources manager scanned me up and down and shook her head. "That kind of outburst in the lunchroom was unacceptable. This is your last and final warning, as your disagreeable attitude has been mentioned several times in the last few months from your supervisor, and your work ethic has decreased as of late. You are suspended without pay for one week and officially put on probation. If your behavior does not improve within a month of your return, we have no choice but to let you go due to poor performance and insubordination."

The entire time she spoke, my chin tightened, and my dead panned locked still on her. I was hot as fuck, but the truth was I needed my job. As much as I wanted to stall the fuck off on the HR manager and my area manager, I couldn't afford to. I didn't have the hustle in me to hit the block and sell drugs or hit the dark web and scam. All I knew how to do was punch a clock. And since I lost Charlie, my motivation to even better myself and actually enroll in the HVAC program had waned. So instead of getting hot, I nodded my head slowly.

"Are we understood?" The HR manager probed.

"Yeah," I seethed.

"Good, now clock out. As a courtesy, you'll receive pay for the entire workday, despite leaving halfway through your shift."

"Thanks!" I sarcastically exclaimed before storming out of the office.

I got to my apartment, which was a fucking drab. It didn't matter that I had new furniture, without a woman's touch, without Charlie's touch entering my place, brought a dread over me so intense that I just wanted to walk back out. Instead, I sat down and started crushing up some weed. There was nothing that a good spliff couldn't take the edge off of. As I inhaled the herb and exhaled a cloudy fog of smoke, all I could think about was how fucked up shit had been since Charlie and I broke up.

Aside from having an apartment that I was struggling to afford, nothing was going right in my life. I was about to be thirty-eight and had no money in the bank. I was busting my ass and breaking my back for seventeen dollars an hour. I had no kids or any real family. It had been ten years since my mother passed away. I never even met my father, and my two brothers were both serving long jail sentences. My older brother Rasheeen was serving twenty-five years to life with a possibility of parole, and my younger brother, Raequan was hit with seventy-eight years. Charlie was the closest person to family. She was the only person

I could rely on. I had to get her back. I had to get her to understand that I needed her. I figured if I just had some alone time to talk with her face-to-face, pour my heart out, and apologize for how I hurt her, there was a possibility that I could get my family back.

It was killing me to know that she was pregnant and most likely the baby was mine but that I had no contact with her. These past few months, I knew she was at Sade's house in Roosevelt Projects, but I couldn't roll up over there with no static. Them niggas in Roosevelt were treacherous. I couldn't survive a war for them niggas, so I stayed away, but now that Charlie was home, it was the perfect time to stake my claim.

My father was a deadbeat, leaving my mother with three young boys to raise. The stress became too much for her to handle, which ultimately drove her to crack. Considering that my father wasn't shit, there was no way I wasn't leaving this earth without being a part of my child's life. My baby deserved a daddy and by any means necessary I would be there.

After smoking two more spliffs, I popped the cap off of an Angry Orchard and downed it in less than a minute. I looked at my phone and it was two o'clock in the morning. My shift was set to end at five a.m., but since I was suspended, and dismissed at around eleven, I didn't get home until a little after midnight. As much as I wanted to head over to Charlie's place right now, I knew it was better to just wait until the morning.

19
SELF-DEFENSE
JADEN

WHILE I WAS TIGHT THAT I COULDN'T STAY AT SEAN and Shelly's condo, nothing beat having a place to call my own. As I woke up and stepped out of bed, stretching and yawning like an old greasy man, a satisfied smile sprung on my face. I was on top of the world, literally, and I had my mother to thank. At first, I was a tad bit upset my mom hadn't gotten me a car, but now I was more grateful to her for turning the apartment over to me in my name. Not only did she do that, but she also redid the entire apartment. Everything I needed was there, from the new plush king-sized bedroom set, stereo system, and a full computer lab.

Even the computer lab, which was decked out with a new desktop and laptop, was finished with photography studio elements. Centered in the corner were a green screen, studio lights, a tripod, and two new Canon cameras. Since I made the decision to take the hybrid position at Vention, New York's leading IT firm, my new work-from-home space would undoubtedly come in handy. And seeing that momma knew that photography was my side hustle, that I wanted to turn into a full fledge business, getting me the necessary equipment to do so was also a plus.

Yeah, a Mercedes Benz made a nigga look good, and I appreciated what Shelly had done, but my momma did what was needed. She helped to put me in a position to be self-sufficient. She set me up to win, and I couldn't thank her more. The bread I dropped on her for Mother's Day a few weeks ago at Ruth Chris was nothing compared to what my mom had done for me. I couldn't be more grateful.

I stumbled into the kitchen, opened the fridge, and pulled out my favorite drink, Tropicana orange juice with some pulp. Momma stocked up on two cases of orange juice from BJs among other stuff. Although she knew I had money to buy my own groceries, she still stocked the house out with food. No one could take my momma's place, not even Shelly, so I hoped her giving me the car and watch was genuine and not a way to get under my momma's skin. Her ass was fat and all, but no one could come between momma and me. I wouldn't allow that.

Nonetheless, I still couldn't get Shelly off my mind. As I downed a gulp of orange juice directly from the jug, I thought about how close Shelly and I were when my momma and Sean left us alone overnight in the condo. We stayed up most of the night smoking Za on the patio, dancing, and talking. Considering that Shelly was older than my momma, of course, she was intelligent and wise, but she also had a playful ditzy side to her that I enjoyed. She was old enough to be my momma, but she didn't act like my momma, so it was easy to like her. And from the way I kept her laughing, I could tell she liked me, especially from how her eyes glowed and her cheeks raised. Ole girl was crushing on me as much as I was crushing on her.

I'ma get her ass one way or another. It's just a matter of time and when.

A firm knock on the door pushed me out of my fantasy. My eyes immediately went to the wall, and I saw it was a little after ten a.m. Seeing as my job started in a few weeks and I just graduated from the pits of eight a.m. courses, I was taking advantage of sleeping in late. Another aggressive knock came as I motioned toward the living room, approaching the door.

Who the fuck was banging on my door this early in the morning? I wasn't expecting any visitors.

"Who is it?" I based up from behind the door, not even bothering to look in the peephole.

"It's Rodney! Open up, Charlie. I know you're in there, and we need to talk."

A mischievous smirk festered from my blood up to my mouth. *This motherfucker had some nerve showing up here.*

"Hold on!" I shrilled, disguising my voice as my momma.

Quickly, I darted into my room, threw a jogger suit on, and slid a blade inside the pocket. I then pulled out a velvet case from under my bed and pulled out my pistol. It was brand new from one of the ranges I frequented in PA. While I had no intention of using the gun, it didn't hurt to bring it for intimidation. I knew for a fact that Rodney's bitch ass wasn't strapped. He probably never even held a hammer before, so this should be easy work.

Before I got back to the door, Rodney had knocked again and was begging like a little bitch. Actually, his cries made him sound like a feign. "Charlie, come on, baby. Open up," he pleaded. Slowly, I opened the door, and there he stood, freshly dressed, with a bouquet of flowers in his hands.

This nigga really thought shit was sweet.

But as soon as he saw my face, his soft simper turned into a cold grimace. "What's up, little nigga? Where's ya momma at?"

From the smirk on his cut-up face and the disregard for my presence, I felt disrespected. Reminded of the many times my momma complained about them fighting, to the bruises I witnessed on her face and neck the last few years that I shrugged off. Momma kept telling me not to worry about him, to leave it alone and allow her to handle it because I had too much to lose, but it was apparent that this nigga wouldn't stop. And if I lost my momma, I would honestly lose everything, including my fucking mind. So, I did what any good son would do. Inching forward, I two-pieced the nigga so hard, knocking the flowers out of his hand and causing him to stumble several feet back.

To my surprise, the nigga regained his composure quickly without falling and charged at me. Busting through the door, he pounced on me, striking me in the head several times. As we wrestled for power, I wrung his neck so tight, determined to choke the breath out of him. Instead, he socked me in the stomach several times, causing me to jump back from him and disappear into the living room. Heavy-footed, Rodney charged after me until we were playing a chasing game around the end table.

Sick of hopping around, I jumped over the table, wrestled him down on the floor, and hit him with a few smooth punches.

"Faggot ass nigga, wanna fight my moms! Fight me, nigga!" I yelled as I repeatedly punched him until blood leaked from his face and his stitches busted open.

He wasn't giving up without a fight, so I stepped back. "Get up, nigga! Fight me since you like to fight! Let's go, nigga," I declared, throwing my hands up and preparing my stance.

I patiently watched him struggle to stand without pouncing on him because I was a fair man. As he staggered, trying to catch his balance, a sinister glow painted his face as he let out a disturbing howl. This nigga was on some spooky shit, and I couldn't play any more games with him, so I pulled my pistol out from my side and aimed it at him.

"Try ya luck, bitch ass nigga, and you gon' see why they call me JD the Trigger."

In a split second, Rodney charged after me like a loose bull and knocked the gun out of my hand. He scrambled on the floor toward it and grabbed hold of the weapon. I ran after him and tried to kick the gun out of his hands, but he tripped me, and I tumbled onto the floor. Rodney's ass was fast, as he hopped on top of me with the barrel of the gun in my face. I couldn't believe this shit. Now he had my fate in his hands, but I couldn't go out like that.

I said a silent prayer in my head as I tried my best not to flinch or make any sudden movements.

"You think you a big guy, huh? So, you a killer, nigga?" he taunted me as blood and spit flew out of his mouth and onto my face.

I remained calm, as I touched for my blade in my pocket.

"You lucky I love your mother, or I would blow your motherfucking head off," he spat. "Now I'm gon' get up and forget any of this ever happened, and we can call this even," he said as he raised up off of me.

Studying his every move, I quickly got up, with my right hand in my pocket. Rodney was a sucker ass nigga, and it was evident from how he was losing it. He dropped the gun on the couch and started pacing back and forth.

"I love your mother. I never meant to hurt her," he rattled.

As he continued blabbering at the mouth, I stepped closer and closer toward the couch.

"I never meant to violate your mother. It's just that I was so mad that she left me, and I couldn't take it, so I took advantage of her. I didn't think anything of it because we had sex so many times before, but now she's pregnant with my baby," he mumbled.

My defenses went up immediately as I processed what he said. "You raped my mother?" I asked as I reached down to grab the gun off the couch.

"I didn't mean to, Jaden. I promise you," he said as he rushed me once he saw me reaching for the gun.

I was sitting on top of the hard steel artillery as he yoked me up, now wringing my neck. As my air supply was narrowing, I reached for the blade in my pocket and slid it into his stomach. At first, he didn't budge, so I nudged the knife deeper and deeper into his groin until he fell flat, breaking the glass end table and his stark red blood, saturating the blade and my hand. Standing over him, I watched as he bled out, staining the hardwood tiles. I shook my head and blew out an exasperated breath.

What the fuck did I just do?

For the next thirty minutes, I paced back and forth in my room as I contemplated what to do and who to call. I hadn't had to kill a nigga since high school, and my weapon of choice was a Glock. Never in my life had I played with knives. I gave a few niggas a Buck50, but I never killed a nigga with no blade. This shit was messy and disturbing as fuck. I stepped back into the living room and watched Rodney's lifeless body lie in a pool of blood. Fidgeting and twiddling the key buttons on my phone, I breathed in and out several times. Luckily, I cleaned my hands so the blood wouldn't stain my phone or ear when I made a call. I couldn't afford to track any of his blood all over the house.

There was no way I could call my mother and explain this to her. Although I was defending her and protecting her honor, I knew that revealing what I had done would bring her a higher level of disgrace. I took a deep breath and did the unthinkable. I dialed Shelly. In less than a minute, she answered.

"Good morning, sweet pea!" she greeted with a chipper tone.

"I need you to come down to the apartment now. It's important. Don't mention it to my mom or Sean."

"Is everything ok, Jaden? Are you all right?" she inquired, panic rising equally with her shaky pitch.

"No questions. Just get here, NOW!"

Watching the clock churn, it seemed like it took forever for Shelly to get here, but it was exactly twenty-four minutes before her knock came to the door. I opened it quickly and was met by confusion written all over her face. Dressed in a fitted denim jumpsuit that hugged her body so well, I almost got distracted from the tragedy just by looking at her.

"What's going on, Jaden? You had me worried!" she shouted.

I pulled her into the house quickly, yanking her by the wrist and slamming the door shut.

"Shh. Keep it down," I warned, holding my index finger against my mouth, letting her know I was serious.

"Look, Shelly. I fucked up, and I didn't know who else to call," I admitted.

Shelly's worried face softened as she looked at me with care. Stepping forward, she placed her hands on my shoulder. "I'm so happy you called me. What's going on, honey?" Her voice was warm, calm, and gentle. She was exactly what I needed in this very instant.

Putting my trust in her, hoping it didn't backfire, I grabbed her by the wrist, leading her into the apartment. As soon as we walked into the living room, she tugged away from my hold and motioned toward the dead body. She approached closer and closer in short, exact movements without saying a word. Once she was up on Rodney, she cursed.

"Rot in hell, bastard!" Shelly seethed as she inhaled deeply and hawked a loud, nasty ball of spit out of her mouth, which landed directly on his face.

Her vile reaction was far from what I expected, throwing me into a frenzy, not knowing what to think.

"Okay, so here's what we're going to do. You're going to call the police. They're going to take you down to the station. DO NOT and I repeat DO NOT say a word. While you're on the phone with the cops, I'll be talking to my lawyer and prepping him on everything, the multiple altercations with your mom, the sexual abuse and him assaulting me. Luckily, your mom reported the rape, so this will all work in our favor. Just make sure you don't say a word to anyone, and I mean anyone. Don't answer any questions, don't accept anything to drink or eat. Just sit tight until your lawyer gets there. His name is Harvey Spencer."

"Okay." I nodded. "Shelly, just please don't tell my mother!"

With earnest and sympathetic eyes, Shelly pursed her lips before saying, "You've got my word!"

20
TRICKY
SHELLY

The cops arrived at Charlie's apartment in less than twenty minutes and Jaden was escorted out uncuffed, which was a relief. The last thing we needed was a spectacle at the apartment, especially when I had to momentarily shield this information from Charlie. Truthfully, it bothered me to hold something so important from Charlie, but I gave Jaden my word and I had to honor that at least until my lawyer got all the necessary details. At that point, if he had to be arraigned and charged, I had no choice but to tell Charlie. There was no way I could keep it from her indefinitely but right now, I had to.

As I watched Jaden enter the unmarked police car, our eyes locked, and I could see the terror in his irises. While he didn't look scared, he looked lost and full of rage. He had just graduated from college. He had such a bright future ahead of him. There was no way he'd have to serve time for this. I couldn't let that happen. I owed it to him and his mother to do everything in my power to ensure that Jaden was able to leave the precinct uncharged and to stay home indefinitely. If not, I wouldn't be able to forgive myself.

"Shelly Fox," I greeted, answering my phone as I watched the police car disappear down the street.

"Good morning, Shelly. I apologize for the delay in returning your call. I just wrapped up a meeting. You said it was urgent. What's going on?"

"I need you to represent someone, Jaden Thompson. A young black male, twenty-one years old. Penn State grad, due to start working at Vention, one of the top IT firms in the city. Possibly murder charge. Self-defense. The victim is his mother's ex-boyfriend, Rodney Kane, who has assaulted her several times and sexually assaulted her. This abuse is documented. The boy and his mother mean a lot to me. The mom, Charlie Thompson, is my girlfriend and employee, and the ex-boyfriend also threatened and attacked me. I need you to get down to the 1st precinct immediately and ask for Jaden Thompson. I'll pay you whatever you request. I just can't let this boy go to jail and throw his life away. I wouldn't be able to forgive myself."

Harvey let out a slow breath. "Got it. I'm on my way. I'll be there in thirty minutes. Make sure you're at the precinct, too. We need to talk face-to-face."

"Understood. I'm on my way as well. I'll be there in ten. See you soon."

The phone hung up and the brisk chilly air hit me on the side of my face. It was a pleasant day in the city, but it felt as if a stone brick was crushing my heart. I hopped into my car and turned the volume dial all the way down. I needed the silence so I could process the wild thoughts running through my mind. While I had only known Jaden for less than two weeks, I felt connected to him and responsible for him. It was killing me slowly to think of all the possibilities that would come with the murder of Rodney. Yeah, Rodney's bitch ass deserved what he got, but would detectives believe Jaden? Would the judge believe him? And would a jury believe him? Would they be able to see past his dreadlocks, intimidating stature, and tattoos that he was a good kid? Or would they dig deep in his expunged record and paint him out to be some kind of menace to society for killing a woman beating rapist?

I was stuck between a rock and a hard place. My loyalty now sided with Jaden, over his mother. I needed him to know he could trust me, and I wanted him to know that I cared for him and believed in him. Although I wanted to tell Charlie, I wasn't prepared for her breakdown. She was pregnant, and I didn't want to overwhelm her by shattering her happiness of just celebrating her son's graduation. Telling her was the right thing, but I couldn't bring myself to do it... at least not right now.

Twenty minutes later, I stormed into the precinct with a determined attitude and my purse tucked under my arm. I needed answers, and I needed them now.

"My son, a tall, African American guy with dreadlocks, was just brought in. Jaden Thompson," I explained to the white officer standing at the front reception area.

He looked me up and down, sizing me up as he folded his arms under his chest. "Your name, ma'am?"

"Shenelle Fox."

"Hmm. Fox. Sounds familiar."

I made it my business to stay calm and not give off any signs that I was bothered as I didn't want to bring any extra attention to myself. I forced a smile on my face, to get him to shut up and give me more information about Jaden.

"What did you say his name was again?"

"Jaden Thompson!" I reiterated.

He nodded his head. "Yeah, he just came in. He requested his lawyer. Now that you're here, he may feel more comfortable talking to our detectives."

I shook my head and pouted, waving my index finger. "Nah, our lawyer is on his way. Just show me to my son, please."

"Your son is not a minor, so you can't be in the room with him. The best I can do is let him know that you're here, while you both wait for his lawyer."

Now I was getting hot. This motherfucker was playing with me!

Instead of displaying my discomfort, I backed off. "No problem. I'll be right here."

I took a seat on the bench and twiddled with my phone. I had a check-in with my rehab counselor where I was required to take a drug test in a few hours. From the way things were going, I knew I wouldn't be able to make it. I pulled up the app and rescheduled my appointment. I knew Sean would be all over me in no time because a part of the outpatient treatment was to have an accountability partner, usually your spouse, who would be notified of all your updates, whether good or bad. Sean would be notified at any second and would call me and question me. I put him on Do Not Disturb, and as soon as I looked up from my phone, in walked Harvey Spencer, one of the best corporate attorneys in the city. Alongside him was a colleague I'd never seen, but I'm sure she'd be the one actually taking the case since Harvey hadn't practiced criminal law in over fifteen years. Still, he was the best, and he always won. Harvey was why our hospital contracts were airtight, and he even closed the deal with the Koch Foundation. There was no person better fit for the job.

"Shelly, nice to see you. Love the new look," Harvey complimented me on the color change to auburn, as he leaned in for a kiss.

"Thanks Harvey."

"No problem, change is always good. Anyway, this is my colleague, one of the top criminal attorneys, Tasnima Motalli. She was featured on *Forbes'* 2020 30 Under 30 Law & Policy Attorneys list. She's one of the best, and she graduated from Howard Law. I know how much you love your alma mater."

I smirked, overwhelmingly impressed as I took Tasnima's hand into mine.

"It's so nice to meet your Mrs. Fox."

"It's nice to meet you, too," I said as I looked into her olive-shaded face, admiring her beautiful cheekbones and clear skin despite her hair being covered in a hijab. Tasnima was a middle eastern woman with a strong Boston accent. It was evident she was born and raised in the States.

"Now that we're all acquainted, sit tight. Tasnima and I will head to the back and get this party started. She's already pulled copies of the order of protection against Rodney Kane and a record of all the assault charges brought against him. This should be a walk in the park, as Jaden's juvenile priors have been expunged from his record, and in the last few years, he's made a great name for himself. Sit tight, we'll be back."

I nodded and watched them walk away, with fear embedded in my heart. While I trusted Harvey and knew that he'd only bring the best criminal attorney to help Jaden, I knew anything was liable to happen when it came to a Black man entangled in the criminal system, especially when you didn't see it coming.

"They're keeping him. He's going to be processed and fingerprinted here. I'll know by tomorrow whether or not the D.A. will file charges. I will try my best to sway the D.A. to consider the recent case of Carlisha Hood and her son in Chicago. Are you familiar?" Tasnima asked.

"Yes, yes. The fourteen-year-old killed a man who attacked his mother. All charges were dropped," I replied.

"Yes, that's the one. I'm hoping that drawing a parallel to that case will work, but the D.A. assigned to this case is a real dickhead with a slight racial motivation against Black men."

A daunting fatigue waved over my body as I exasperated. "Great," I sarcastically mumbled.

Harvey placed his heavy hand on my shoulder. "Don't worry. I'm familiar with the D.A. I'll talk to him. By the way, your husband knows him better than me. Although he is a bit of a racist, he's also a well-known Mason. Sean has been a guest of his every year at the annual New York Bar Association Gala."

"Great," I repeated with even more sarcasm. "I'll talk with Sean as soon as I get home."

"Good and tell him Sean I said hello."

"Will do," I affirmed to Harvey. "I'll be waiting for your call, Tasnima," I added before watching them walk away.

21
SORRY
SHELLEY

"**W**HY DID YOU PUSH YOUR DRUG TEST BACK?"
Sean roared as soon as I set foot inside the condo. Charlie, whose belly looked like it had grown bigger overnight was laid out across the couch.

"Sheesh, can I sit down and get a glass of water first before you start jumping down my throat," I responded as I side-eyed him, with a glint of irritation.

"No, you can't. I'm paying top dollar for you at the best private outpatient rehab in the city, making sure you're secure and comfortable. I need to know what the fuck is going on."

"It's nothing! I just didn't feel like it. As you know, I was smoking with Jaden, so that will come up, so I figured I'd do a flush out before getting tested."

"How fucking convenient. How can I be sure you aren't still skiing on coke and using weed as a coverup?" Sean's accusation was riddled with assault, as his voice and pitch were full of violence.

I already wasn't having the best day, having to hold Jaden's secrets and bottle up my emotions and Sean was pushing me to the limit.

"Because I'm your wife and you should trust me!"

Sean's cheeks pushed his eyebrows up as a nasty grimace painted his mouth. "Shelly, fuck you. You always want to throw the wife card around for your benefit. It's obvious that I can't trust you unless we wouldn't be in this situation in the first place."

Standing to her feet, Charlie waved her hands dismissively. "Look, stop the bullshit, Sean. Shelly's going through a lot right now. She literally just walked in the door and you're grilling her. Let's just relax, have some dinner, and watch something funny on TV. Katt Williams and Monique just dropped Netflix specials."

Charlie had saved the day with her suggestion, and I couldn't be happier. I walked over to her and wrapped my arms around her before planting a kiss on her forehead. "Thank you," I whispered.

"No problem." She smiled, her voice soothing, leaving a calming impression on me and my troubling thoughts.

Just as I thought I could escape the realities of today's unfortunate events, I was reminded of the burden weighing heavy on my soul.

"Shelly, have you heard from Jaden? He hasn't answered his phone all day. I don't want to have to pop up on his ass to let him know I don't care how grown his ass is. He's not to ignore my calls for hours."

It was now or never. I had to say something, although I was mentally exhausted and just wanted to shower.

Instead of answering her directly, I walked away and headed into the kitchen.

"Shelly, do you not hear me talking to you?" Charlie's voice echoed behind me. "Will you believe her?" Charlie asked.

"I've stopped believing her some time ago," Sean said, his voice low but still audible enough for me to hear even in the kitchen.

Opening the fridge, I pulled out an unopened bottle of Sweet Bitch, my favorite affordable choice of sweet wine. Untwisting the bottle, I grabbed a glass and poured a full cup. As I turned around, Charlie was staring at me with her hands on her hips.

"I know when something's not right, and the fact that you walked away from me mid-conversation gives me the inclination that you're hiding something. Where the fuck is my son?"

I downed half of my glass and enjoyed the sweet taste of red wine before I faced the music.

"Jaden was arrested this morning. He promised me not to tell you, which is why I sent my lawyer, one of the best in the city down to the precinct to represent him."

With her chin pointed in the air, I could see Charlie's nostrils flaring and a tightness in her eyes.

"You promised him not to tell me? JADEN IS MY SON, SHELLY, NOT YOURS! I don't care what fancy bullshit you try to shower him with! He's MY SON!" she hollered.

As I formed the words to say, Sean peered into the kitchen. "What's going on?"

"Jaden was arrested this morning, and Superwoman Shelly has been to the precinct already and hired him a lawyer without telling me," she replied, looking directly at Sean.

"And yet you want us to trust you?" Sean sassed as his lips rose into a mischievous smile.

Sean was using everything against me, and it didn't help that he had a teammate to help beat me up.

"Charlie, I was going to tell you once I found out if the D.A. would be pressing charges. I didn't want to bother you with this horrific news. You're pregnant and dealing with a lot already," I explained, my voice straining for understanding.

Charlie stepped closer to me. "You don't get to decide what is too much for me, especially when it comes to my son. Now spill it! What was he arrested for?"

Inside, my pulse sped up faster than I expected. "Murder."

Charlie's eyes bulged. Her shoulders collapsed as she dropped her head. "Murder? And you weren't going to tell me?" she roared.

"Take me to the precinct now! I need to see my son!"

"I don't think that's a good idea right now, Charlie. You're upset. Emotions are high, and anything you guys talk about can and will be used against you. Just sleep this off because if he's indicted, you'll be involved anyway," I said.

Balling up her fists, Charlie stepped closer and closer in my face until our stomachs were touching each other. Looking down at her, I exhaled, allowing a light breath to roll out of my mouth. I was not prepared for this.

"Shelly, you're going to tell me exactly what happened, from start to finish. From the moment you got a phone call from my son to the moment he was arrested. Now start talking!" she demanded.

I backed up slowly, yearning for personal space, and Charlie followed my every step. As I glanced up at Sean, he was standing with his left arm holding his right elbow while cupping his chin. His brickstoned face was solid and quiet as a rock. I was being attacked in my own home and felt all alone, even with my husband in the same room, after I brought this woman into my home and life.

"This morning, I got a call from Jaden, telling me he needed me to come down to the apartment and not to tell you. I rushed down there, and when I got inside the apartment, Rodney was lying in a pool of blood on the floor."

Charlie covered her mouth in shock, and Sean wrapped her in his arms. A soft cry pelted from Charlie. "My baby! Oh my god! My baby boy, no! I can't believe this! It's all my fault!" she cried.

I approached them and lowered my head to Charlie. "No, no, it's not your fault. Rodney came to the house, and a fight pursued. Jaden was defending himself."

"It's all my fault! It's all my fault! I should have had Rodney arrested! I should have protected my baby! He said if he saw Rodney, he was going to kill him. I should have made sure that Rodney was behind bars. Now my baby will probably spend the rest of his life in jail!" Tears were streaming down Charlie's face, and her bright eyes looked like the Red Sea.

With as much pain as I had seen Charlie in, I had never witnessed her in this much distress. She was breaking in front of my eyes. Weeping, she started to lose her balance, so I reached out to grab her up, and she pushed me away.

"Don't touch me, Shelly! Don't fucking touch me! I don't care what my son said! You should have immediately called me!"

Rocking slightly and chewing on my inner cheeks, I dragged my palms down my face. "I'm sorry, Charlie. I just didn't know what to do."

"You're always sorry, and frankly, I'm tired of hearing it. From now on, stay out of it. I'll call Harvey and find out which of his colleagues he stuck on this. I may know the D.A., and if it's who I think it is, these charges may be dropped immediately," Sean said before grabbing Charlie's face in his hands. "Don't worry, baby, everything is going to be okay. Jaden is coming home," he assured as he kissed Charlie deeply and whisked her out of the room.

I stood in my kitchen drinking the rest of my wine with a feeling of emptiness on the inside. *How in the hell had it come to this? How in the hell was my husband falling out of love with me and falling in love with a woman he'd never look at twice, like Charlie? What the fuck did I do to my marriage by introducing Charlie into it?*

22

LEMONS TO LEMONADE
CHARLIE

MY PRESSURE WAS HIGH, AND THE MIGRAINE PULS-ing through my head was nearly unbearable. I couldn't sleep. I couldn't even eat. Despite how much Sean tried to force me to get something on my stomach, I could barely keep it down. Of course, all he cared about was the unborn baby I was carrying, not knowing that all I cared about was the baby I'd raised into a young man.

As we sat inside the courtroom, waiting for the arraignment to start, my palms were sweating, watching all the lawyers and their clients huddle together in secrecy. I flipped my head back and forth, looking for my baby, but he was nowhere to be found.

"Don't worry, baby. I told you everything is going to be alright. I spoke with the D.A. yesterday. Trust me, that's all I'm asking is for you to trust me. I told him everything about your past, the sexual abuse, having a child at thirteen, the assaults from Rodney, and how good of a kid Jaden is. Trust me. They are dropping the charges," Sean asserted with so much confidence it kind of pissed me off.

While my racing heartbeat had slowed down, my defenses were still up. I never trusted law enforcement, and as much as I appreciated Sean and even Shelly, Jaden was my son. They didn't have children, so they had no idea what I was going through. Both of them wanted so badly to fix everything, thinking it could just all go away, but I knew better than that.

Whether Sean or Shelly knew it, I still had to live with the guilt that my son killed a man because of me. I had to sleep with that shit on my conscious every night. My abuser may be dead, but the pain, an even deeper pain, especially if my son had to pay, would be exacerbated.

I stayed mute, watching the court attendees, trying my best not to look Sean or Shelly's way, who were both seated on each side of me. I didn't want to hear a peep out of them. I just wanted my son to come home. As I rubbed my belly, trying to quiet down my emotions for the baby I was carrying, I saw my son dressed in a jogger suit with hand-cuffs wrapped around his wrists.

My emotions heightened again as I stood up from my seat. "Jaden, baby! Momma is here!" I shouted out.

Jaden turned his head along with the court attendees and looked at me. A big Kool-Aid smile brushed his face as he nodded his head in my direction.

"Ma'am, please do not scream in here again, or I will have to escort you out," one of the court officers standing by the edge of the bench closest to Shelly's side warned.

"She's sorry, officer. It won't happen again." Sean leaned forward to look the overweight white officer in the eyed. The officer nodded his head in recognition and turned away.

Moments later, a strange quietness fell over the courtroom. I raised my head and saw a white judge heading to his seat.

"All rise, the court is now in session with Honorable Matthews presiding. Please be seated, the bailiff announced.

As the mafia boss-looking judge whispered to the bailiff while going through several manila folders, my knees started to shake. I didn't know what to expect. Sean noticed my nervousness and rested his hand gently on my thigh.

"Thompson vs. The State of New York," the judge announced while flicking his slick hair out of his face. From his oily skin and thick Italian accent, I wouldn't be surprised if he was cast in the *Sopranos*, that is, if he weren't the judge that would be responsible for my son's demise.

I watched as my baby boy raised his head, straightened his back, and took his stance before the judge. My heart was thumping as I held my breath, unprepared for the worst and hoping for the best.

"District Attorney Tim Camp for the State of New York, and my co-counselor, Sherrie Crenshaw."

"That's my guy, baby. He's going to do the right thing," Sean whispered in my ear as he huddled me in his embrace, his arm wrapped around my neck.

"Good morning, Your Honor. Tasnima Motalli is representing Jaden Thompson."

"Mr. Thompson, you've been charged with murder in the first degree of Rodney Kane, a Class A felony and punishable by up to life in prison.

Mr. Thompson, how do you plead?"

"Not guilty!" Jaden pledged.

"Your Honor, the charge against my client should be completely dismissed on the grounds of self-defense. Jaden was protecting his property and, most importantly, defending his mother's honor when the deceased approached him at his residence for a fight. It is also on record that the deceased has physically assaulted my client's mother several times and, most recently, sexually assaulted her. Lastly, the deceased was even stalking my client's mother at her home and at work, which caused her to take a leave of absence from her job and even move out and turn over her apartment to my client. None of that, including a police-issued order of protection, stopped the deceased from continuing to stalk Jaden's mother, trespass into her building, and pick a fight with my client while pursuing my client's mother. And yes, I submitted all police reports and the signed order of protection to your office yesterday," the Middle Eastern lawyer iterated.

"Honorable Matthews, there is no way that my office can sign on a dismissal of all charges when a man was brutally murdered, especially on the basis of self-defense. The defense's argument should be tried in court for a jury to hear the bloody details of the final moments of Rodney Kane's life. Then, it can be determined from an unbiased jury if self-defense is warranted," the co-counselor bitch countered.

I elbowed Sean in the side and crunched my face as I fumed. "What happened to your man handling things? He's letting this bitch railroad my son!" I vehemently barked, my volume low yet intense, as I vilely eyed Sean.

"Relax, relax. It's not over yet. Tim knows what he's doing," Sean defended him as he tried to kiss me on the forehead, but I scooted away from him so fast.

The judge waved his head from side to side, looking at both the D.A., then Jaden and his lawyer. Silence dawned over the courtroom as the judge pondered his decision.

"After a thorough look at the police reports, it is clear the deceased was not a good Samaritan and has inflicted much harm on the plaintiff's mother. With that said, the charges will be lessened to manslaughter in the second degree. However, I agree with the D.A. that the plaintiff's fate must be determined by a jury who can mull over the fine details to determine if self-defense holds up. The trial starts on September 12th. Seeing that there is no cash bail or pretrial detention required under the new bail reform law for manslaughter in the second degree, you are free to go, Mr. Thompson. However, you are prohibited from traveling out of the state or the country. This court is adjourned!" The judge hit his gavel, finalizing the case, and the court officer removed the handcuffs from Jaden's wrists.

"Come on, y'all. Let's go," Shelly said as she stood from her seat. Sean and I both followed her out of the courtroom.

As soon as I saw Jaden, I grabbed him into a tight embrace and refused to let go. Faint tears trickled down my face as he held me even tighter. "Baby, I'm so sorry."

"Ma, stop apologizing. You have nothing to be sorry about. He deserved it, and if I had to, I'd do it again."

"No baby, please don't talk like that. I told you. I don't want you fighting my battles. You have too much good happening in your life. I wouldn't be able to live with myself, knowing I fucked your life up before it even got started."

Jaden let me go, and I was reminded we weren't in our own little bubble. Shelly and Jaden's lawyer were huddled around us. As I looked to my right, Sean was talking with the D.A. down the hall.

"Momma, it's nothing you can tell me that would stop me from ever protecting you because what you don't understand is that you are my life, and without you, I have nothing," Jaden gravely replied.

More tears flowed, and I hugged him again. "I love you, baby."

"I love you more, momma," he expressed as he kissed me on the forehead and let me go again. He then grabbed me by the hand and started to walk. Looking at his lawyer, Jaden nodded his head forward.

The lawyer and Shelly both headed in our direction toward the elevators. The courthouse halls were pretty empty, as most of the morning sessions had just gotten started.

"Thank you both so much," Jaden asserted, looking at Shelly and the lawyer.

"You're welcome, Jaden," the lawyer responded. "Hi, Ms. Thompson, my name is Tasnima, and I am happy to represent your son," she said, extending her hand.

My eyes trailed from her face to her neck and then her hand. I took my time grabbing it.

"I know you may be a little distrusting, but I assure you that I am going to do everything in my power to ensure that Jaden beats trial and won't have to spend a day in jail," Ms. Motalli proclaimed.

"And so am I," Sean's voice trailed in. I turned around and saw him standing there. "Sean Fox, nice to meet you. Harvey Spencer is a very close friend of mine," he said, extending his hand to her.

They exchanged handshakes, and she smiled.

"The D.A. is another close friend of mine who is friends with the judge. They are on our side. He just couldn't move for dismissal at this hearing. The co-counselor pushed for a trial, knowing that the judge would drop the murder charge to second-degree manslaughter, allowing Jaden to come home today. The D.A. assured me that his office would review the reports and get the charges dropped before trial. He just has some work to do," Sean explained.

Tasnima nodded her head while we all looked at Sean in awe.

"Well, you stay out of trouble, Jaden, and remember, no traveling out of state, not even to Jersey," Tasnima reminded as he held onto Jaden's hand.

"Will do. Thank you again."

"No problem. Enjoy your day with your family. We'll talk soon," Tasnima said before walking away.

23
TAKE CARE
JADEN

"*Now that our apartment is an active crime scene, you have no other option but to stay here at the condo with us," my mother explained as Shelly, Sean, and I sat on the sofa looking at her and her growing pregnant belly. Seeing as she was the shortest person amongst us, it appeared that she stood while she talked to assert some form of authority. She clearly wanted us to know that she was serious.*

"I'm sorry to cramp your style, ma, but thank you. And thanks Sean and Shelly for everything. I know I haven't known either of you for long, but thank you for making me feel like family," I expressed whole-heartedly.

Sean bounced his knee twice and rubbed his hands together. "You are family, Jaden. By the way, I want to take you out soon. We can have a little guy time and introduce you to some of my frat brothers."

A calm smile flew up the corners of my mouth. "That sounds good. Thanks."

"Thank you, Sean," momma said.

"Speaking of going out, I want to take you suit shopping. You start at Vention on Monday, and you need to be sharp for the top IT firm in the city," Shelly offered.

I slapped my hand on my forehead and huffed. "With everything happening, I forgot all about that. You're right. I do need to go shopping."

"Great, Sean call Donna down at Michael Andrews and tell her we're coming in," Shelly ordered.

"Got it!" Sean replied.

Momma folded her arms and leveled all of her weight on her right hip. "Shelly, I'd prefer to take my son shopping for his work suits. Just give me the address, and I'll get us there," my momma interjected.

"Don't be ridiculous, Charlie. You're five months pregnant, and your feet are swollen," Sean butted in, causing me to look down at my momma's oversized feet, and he was right.

Pouting, my momma switched her stance to her other hip. "Well, why don't you take him? This is more of a man thing, anyway."

"Generally, it is, but Shelly picks out all of my suits, anyway. I just show up to get them fitted, so she would be the best person to take Jaden," Sean argued.

I sat back in my seat with a devious smirk, bouncing my eyes from Sean and my momma. This nigga was practically giving his wife away, which was cool by me. All that meant was I had more time to spend with Shelly up close and personal.

"Sorry, Charlie, shopping is what I do best, and Sean knows it. So how about you and Sean head to the chiropractic spa and get an adjustment, a foot massage, or even a mud bath? You're pregnant, babe, and all three of us are here to serve you. So, relax and enjoy," Shelly cooed as the corners of her lips rose into a sweet simper.

Damn, she was sexy even when she wasn't trying.

Two hours later, Shelly and I rolled into Michael Andrews, one of the most expensive premier suit boutiques in New York, according to Google. It even smelled like money in there.

"Shelly, it's so nice to see you," a natural redhead, white woman who looked like a much older version of Ice Spice, stated.

"It's nice to see you too, Donna," Shelly greeted her as they exchanged kisses on the cheek. "This is Jaden, a friend of the family. He starts a new job at Vention, one of the top IT firms in the city. He needs a monthly supply of suits. I'm thinking twenty to start with."

Donna poked out her lips and bounced her head three or four times. "Makes sense. He can spread them out amongst other business casual looks for the next three months and make a really great impression. I got it." Donna shot her trigger finger at Shelly and smirked. "Why don't you follow me over here so we can get your inseams," she directed.

"Ladies first!" I exclaimed, then winked at Shelly.

She giggled and sashayed in front of me, her thick ass gyrating in her form fitted skirt. My eyes were glued to her shape, so much that Donna caught me looking. Donna's raised eyebrows and rapid jaw movement told me I needed to chill, so I did.

"Eddie, full measurements for this young fella, here," Donna instructed an old man dressed in one of the best suits I'd ever seen. It fit him so well, and it took at least ten years off of him, I assumed because although he was up there in age, he was spiffy and mobile.

"I'm going to pull you a few pieces from the front. Shelly, make sure he's got the right fit."

"You got it," Shelly responded to Donna, smacking her lips, which caused my mind to swirl in a frenzy as I thought about what those lips could do.

Fantasizing about Shelly posed a huge distraction from the fact that I was facing manslaughter charges. While I had faith in what Sean told us about the D.A. there was still a lingering doubt in the back of my mind. Shopping and spending the day with Shelly felt great and was exactly what I needed to keep my mind from trailing into negative thoughts.

"Pants and sweatshirt off. Stand up here," Eddie instructed, pointing to the elevated stand situated in front of the mirrors.

I took no time to throw off my sweatshirt and drop my pants. My boxer briefs were well-fitted, showing my thick bulge. As I motioned near the mirrors, I caught Shelly's mouth open as she eyed my print. She licked her lips slowly as her eyes traveled down my back, then to my dick again. Our eyes met as she looked past me into the mirror, and the intensity thickened like a left-out bowl of oatmeal. My chest hairs rose, and Shelly's nipples hardened like rocks through her blouse as we stared each other down.

"It's getting hot in here, folks. Let me remind Donna to turn up the air," Eddie jested as a sly laugh rolled out of his mouth.

The fact that he caught us flirting made us both laugh.

While we had company cramping our style, it didn't stop our eyes from undressing each other. I may have been partially naked, but I could tell from how softly Shelly bit her lips and how her mouth watered that she wanted to see my whole package and from the way my mischievous pout sat on the edge of my smirk and how my eyebrow bounced up occasionally, I knew, she knew I wanted her, and she knew I knew she wanted me.

There was just something about Shelly that I couldn't put my finger on, but it was killing me to uncover. As much as I didn't want to fuck up the relationship that I was building with Sean, I was more so interested in what could become of his wife and me. And as the saying goes, you make a choice, take a chance, and reap the consequences, good or bad.

"Wakey, wakey! Wake up!"

My eyes opened to Shelly standing over me and planting a kiss on my cheek.

"It's your first day of work."

I can't believe the weekend went by that fast.

I leaned up in the bed, wiped the cold out of my eye and stretched my arms. Getting a clearer vision of Shelly, she was wearing a silk robe tied tight with her breasts boasting to pop out.

"What time is it?" I asked, confused by the darkness outside of the window.

"Four o'clock in the morning," she answered.

I inhaled deeply and a whiff of cinnamon hit my nostrils. "You cooking?"

"No, your momma is, so get yourself up. It's your first day, so you need to get a quick workout in with Sean, eat, then get showered and dressed. Work starts at eight a.m., so you need to be there no later than seven thirty. Capuche?" Shelly said, her voice all feisty and flirty.

"Capuche."

Shelly stood back from the bed and allowed me to admire her long legs. There was so much unspoken tension between us, and it seemed like every day, despite how crazy and unexpected, our chemistry continued to build. I felt like I was in a movie. I couldn't believe my mother was in a poly relationship, and her girlfriend and I were digging each other. The shit was getting weirder by the day.

"Well, what are you waiting for? Sean will be by the door in ten minutes to head to the gym. Get moving!" she forcefully ordered before disappearing from my room.

By the time I washed my face, brushed my teeth, and threw on some basketball shorts and a wife beater, a knock came on my door. In walked Sean dressed in a full suit.

"I thought we were working out?"

"I can't. I have a seven o'clock breakfast with the Newark Regional Business Partnership at the Robert Treat Hotel. It's one of the chambers of commerce that the hospital is a part of, so I have to swing by the office for a quick meeting and then head to Jersey."

I nodded my head, impressed by how well put together Sean was. I kind of felt bad for lusting after his wife, but he was fucking my mother and his wife. It was obvious he didn't mind sharing.

"Anyway, I came by to bring you this." Sean pulled out a cherry red velvet box from the inside of his suit jacket. He handed me the box with a bright, beaming smile.

The word *DIAMONDERE* was spelled out across the face of the box. I opened it, and there were two silver studs with blue diamonds in the middle. They were dope but not really my style. I wasn't an earring-wearing type of nigga.

Due to my widened eyes and silence, Sean smiled. "They're cufflinks from the best company on the market. They're sapphires around the 14-karat white gold with VVS diamonds. A man of your stature should never step foot into one of the top IT firms wearing a Michael Andrews suit without cufflinks. I wanted to personally give them to you before I headed out."

Damn. The Fox's were really loaded, and Sean was a good nigga. I couldn't accept all of his gifts and kindness and still try to fuck his wife. That was just low, and I was sure that a relationship with Sean would be more beneficial to me in the long run. I had to cut the flirting with Shelly. It wasn't cool, and I couldn't do that to Sean. He was too good to my momma and me.

"Wow, thank you. I appreciate you, boss, for everything. For showing a young nigga like me a different side of life and just being so open to me," I sincerely expressed.

Sean raised his chin high as he thrust his chest out. A knowing grin accompanied a head nod, as he grazed me with direct and intense eye contact. "It's no problem, man. You don't know how much I've always wanted a son. Having you around is going to be great. I'm really looking forward to getting to know you more," he said with a gleam in his eye that showed respect.

Sean looked at me like a man, like I was his equal, yet with a protective air I had never experienced, as my parents broke up when I was too young to understand what having a loving father really meant.

I was lost for words. All I could do was sweep Sean into a warm hug. He hugged me back, probably never knowing that my own father had never embraced me.

After eating breakfast and getting good wishes from Shelly and my momma for my first day, I hopped in my Mercedes Benz and made my way toward Midtown. Thank God, I was able to get my car back from the apartment, the other day, so I could cruise into work like the player I was. Cruising down the West Side Highway with my top down, blowing a spliff, it just seemed like life was lit.

Once I pulled into the underground parking lot of the building on Broadway and 21st Street, I found my parking spot in the visiting area. By the end of the day, I was sure that I would have my permanent parking pass. As I sprayed down the car and myself, with Febreze then added a touch of Baccarat behind my eyes, I looked at myself in the mirror. I looked good and my cufflinks were shining on my navy-blue suit. *I was the man.*

I hopped out of the car and made my way inside the building to the reception area.

"Jaden Thompson. Today is my first day at Vention," I explained to the security guard behind the desk of one of the most modernesque lobbies I'd come across. It was obvious they had some renovations within the last few years.

"Give me a second. Let me phone the receptionist upstairs."

While he got on the phone, I eyed the lobby, taking in all the architectural accents of the building. It was architecture porn, appeasing my passion for structural buildings. When in college, I thought of taking up the architecture program, but it was six years, so I declined. I wanted to get out of school in four years, nothing more, and seeing as I started college at seventeen years old, I wouldn't be turning twenty-two years old until later in the year.

"Take the first elevator on your right to the sixteenth floor," the guard instructed.

"Thanks. By the way, man, what's your name?"

The guard smirked and shook his head disbelievingly. "It doesn't matter. Have a good day, sir," he dismissively replied.

I walked away irritated but refused to let that asshole fuck up my day. I stepped off the elevator and two large glass doors with the words *Vention* on them stood in front of me. Before I could open the door, a white woman dressed in a pantsuit exited. She was short, almost dwarf-like, and her long ponytail rode on her waist.

"Jaden?"

"Yes, good morning. It's so nice to meet you," I said, extending my hand for a handshake that she declined. Her eyes didn't even travel down my hand. She looked up at me with no inch of emotion.

Embarrassed, I pulled my hand back and settled them in my pants pocket.

"We are sorry to inform you that your offer with Vention has been withdrawn, in light of the manslaughter indictment you've been charged with. While our great country honors the adage 'innocent until proven guilty', our company chooses not to employ any employees with such gross allegations against them. My HR director will be emailing and mailing you a separation agreement for your records. We truly do wish you the best. Take care, Jaden."

24
BLOODY
SHELLY

FOR SOME REASON, I WAS HORNIER THAN A MOTHER-fucker since I hadn't officially returned to work. My nipples were hard, and my pussy was begging for some tender loving care. Sean and I hadn't had sex in a while. Shit, since we attended Jaden's graduation, nobody was getting any action. And things hadn't gotten any better since Jaden moved in with us a week ago. I usually wasn't attracted to young guys, but what Jaden and I had was different. He admired me in an innocent way. He allowed me to let my hair down, yet he was so intellectual that we could talk for hours. He brought out a youthful side of me that I needed right now, especially since things were still rocky with Sean and me, and Charlie was also pulling away from me. I knew that in a matter of time, Sean would be all over Charlie and the baby, leaving me on the outs. I wasn't really prepared for that, and the more I looked at Charlie when Sean showered her with affection, envy grew in my heart.

Pushing the negative thoughts out of my head, I was reminded that I had the house to myself since Jaden, Sean, and Charlie were at work. I cocked my legs open onto the bed, prepared to lull my clit to surrender. As soon as I stuck my middle finger into my center, the extra wetness alarmed me. I pulled my finger out, and it was full of blood.

What the fuck? I haven't gotten my period since last October.

Since I had irregular periods, I barely experienced PMS symptoms, so I never knew when my period was on its way. No backaches, no bloating, or pelvic pain came prior. Nonetheless, as I thought about my last period, I remembered that it was torturous with headaches, body aches, and cramps, so if I had to base it on that, this period was bound to be difficult.

I jumped up from the bed and examined the sheets. Thank God, no blood. I went into the bathroom to jump in the shower but noticed I needed two new rags, so I tiptoed out of the bedroom, heading straight for the laundry room. As I entered the laundry room, the intercom from the reception area rang. Confused as to who it could be, I scrunched my brows and headed toward the digital intercom in the kitchen. I tapped on the touchscreen and saw Jaden standing with his head down and his dreads covering his face.

"Jaden?" I questioned into the intercom.

His shoulders rolled back as he lifted his face. His eyes were dark, and he barely moved as he stood stone steel with his face in the camera. I buzzed him in instantly and ran into the bathroom to throw on a thin pad and some sweats. By the time I did that, there was a knock at the door. I rushed forward and opened it to a broken Jaden, whose eyes were watery.

"What happened, Jaden? What happened? Are you alright?" I shouted, completely confused as to what had made him so distraught.

He stumbled through the door, dropped his bag, and wrapped me in his arms. He held me so tight without saying a word. The sound of muffled, soft cries filled the room. I stroked his back as he held me tighter and tighter. His touch was comforting, unlike Sean's, which was forced these last few months.

"Jaden, baby. Please talk to me. I'm worried," I managed to say again.

He finally let me go and raised his head to look at me. Sniffling, he managed to say, "Vention let me go. They heard about the manslaughter charges. My future is ruined. Shit is just so fucked up. Momma was right."

I dragged my hands down my face and let out a long breath. "It's okay, it's okay," I assured, pulling Jaden by the hand, toward the couch.

I sat down, and he followed behind me. Taking his hand into mine, I said," Don't worry. Your charges will be dismissed in no time, and you'll be able to return to your everyday life. In the meantime, Sean and I can get you a job in the IT department at the hospital. It may not be the kind of work you were looking for right now, but the pay and benefits are competitive with the industry's standards," I explained.

I just wanted Jaden to know that he had options, and whatever I could do to help him, I would. Resting my hand on his thigh, I remained quiet, allowing my words to marinate and for him to soak them up. Instead, he circled his index finger around my hand until it trickled up to my collarbone, and he grabbed me by the neck. His touch made me quiver, and my heart jumped a beat. As his palm rested on my chest, we locked eyes, and I knew that what we were about to do could never be undone once we crossed that line.

Jaden slid closer to me and kissed me deeply and passionately. In less than one minute, he was sucking on my neck, fondling my breasts, and pulling my shirt off. I allowed him to caress me, sending shocks up my spine. His firm hands gripped my ass as he slid inside my panties. I squeezed my thighs tight, remembering that I was on my period. His bothered eyes challenged me as he silently questioned my restriction. He didn't care, though. He instead pried my legs open and motioned his fingers around my clit slowly, causing me to shake. He bit his lips and lowered his eyes, watching me enjoy his hands. Yanking my sweatpants down until they were off, he pulled his hand up and eyed his bloody fingers. To my shocking surprise, he licked both of his fingers and inched closer, and kissed me again. It was the nastiest, filthiest thing I ever did. We were one in the flesh.

As we continued to kiss, I heard Jaden unbuckle his belt and felt him wiggle out of his pants. His large dick slapped across my thigh, causing me to shrill, and his immediate devilish chuckle put me at ease, until he slid inside me so smoothly. His dick massaged my insides as he humped slowly, slipping and sliding in and out of me.

"Oh yes," I moaned, overwhelmed from the pleasure, as I've never had sex on my menstrual but something about it felt better than before. I was also hornier and wetter than usual.

Jaden continued to stroke and stroke at a slow, steady pace, which he broke up with an occasional hard thrust. I looked up, watching him bite his lips. Pleasure was written all over his face as we locked eyes, and he lowered his head, planting a warm kiss on my forehead. The sound of his smooch turned me on even more, causing my pussy walls to pulsate and wrap tighter around his dick.

He planted his fists on each side of me, lowered himself deeper and did several pushups in my pussy. Him being so close to me and still being able to drill inside of me, confirmed just how much dick his young ass was carrying around. Wanting to feel all of him, I wrapped my legs around his torso, and he placed his hands under my lower back and snuggled in between the crevices of the warmest place on earth. He sped up his tempo, power-drilling me, and splashing through my pretty red sea.

He held back his moans, but from the intensity of his grunts, I knew he was enjoying me. And from the way my eyes rolled into the back of my head, he knew I was enjoying him. The way my pussy was talking surprised me. I couldn't believe I was fucking someone nearly twenty years younger than me, and I was actually enjoying it.

As Jaden dug deeper and deeper, this time caressing my right thigh in the air, I hyperventilated, trying to catch my breath, but he took it from me. He kissed me from my ankle all the way down my leg until he plastered his lips onto mine, and we kissed slowly, pecking, and nibbling seductively until we came in unison. Even after his cum orbited my nectar, his dick stiffened, and he swam through me for what had to be over an hour before I came again and again.

25
SILVER LINING
CHARLIE

"*Isn't there something we can do?" I asked* aloud but really directed my statement to Sean.

We were all seated at the kitchen island having breakfast. Shelly and Jaden were at one end of the island and Sean, and I were at the other end.

"From my knowledge of employment law, I'm afraid we can't. They let him go before he started, and most IT companies don't hire felons."

"But I'm not a felon. I have not been convicted yet," Jaden argued, his pitch high and full of frustration.

"Exactly," I joined in defending my baby.

"I know. I know. You're right. I'm sorry!" Sean apologized.

"Have you heard anything from the D.A. yet, Sean?"

"No, and I wouldn't. The D.A. should be communicating directly with Harvey's girl, the lawyer on the case. What's her name?"

"Tasnima," Shelly answered as she cut a slice of pancake and stuffed it into her mouth.

"Yeah, she should be calling Jaden any day now," Sean noted.

I took a sip of my hot brewing coffee and rubbed my belly. So far, the pregnancy was actually taking a calm turn. My morning sickness had subsided, and now I was just feeling heavy, tired, and occasionally dealing with swollen feet.

"Whew, baby, slow down on that coffee. You know the doctor said you can't have more than eight ounces, and that's a big mug," Sean warned in a badgering manner.

"The doctor said no more than one and a half cups, and this is my first one and I haven't even finished it. Relax!" I corrected.

"When's your next checkup, anyway?" Shelly inquired.

"It was yesterday," Sean answered.

Shelly stuck her neck out and crinkled her brows. "Yesterday? And you guys went without me?" Shelly roared, looking directly at Sean.

"It's really not even necessary for you to attend the appointments. This is my and Charlie's baby," Sean asserted, which even stung me a bit.

I continued to sip my coffee because the tension was getting thick, and I didn't know what to do or say. Instead, I studied Jaden's face as he grew defensive. He even put his hand on Shelly's shoulder. It was early June, about a week before Father's Day, and Jaden had only been around for about a month, yet he and Shelly had grown awfully close. I saw the way he looked at her, and at first I dismissed it, just chalking it up to his raging hormones and him being a young man. Shelly was fine as fuck. Even I knew that, but there was something about the protective gleam in his eye as Shelly expressed her displeasure that got me thinking.

"You and Charlie's baby, huh? But I'm your—"

"Yes, I know. You're my wife, but you're not the mother of my unborn child. So how about you stay in your lane and let Charlie and I do the parent thing? Okay, babe?" Sean sarcastically chided as his tongue clacked against his teeth.

Just before Shelly could respond, Jaden interrupted. Holding up his vibrating phone, he said, "My lawyer's calling."

"Answer it, boy, and put it on speaker," I demanded.

"Hello!" Jaden shouted.

"Good morning, Jaden. I have some good news for you. The D.A. and I came together to file a motion for dismissal of the charges, and the judge just signed off on it without the necessity of a hearing. I need you to come down here and sign these papers to acknowledge your discharge of custody and travel stipulations."

Jaden's face lit up with joy as he hopped up from the seat. "What time?"

"Can you be down here at One Centre Street in an hour?"

"Hell yeah. I'll see you shortly. Thank you so much!" Jaden expressed before hanging up.

"Well, that was quick," Sean stated.

"It wasn't quick enough to save me my job. Now I have to reach back out to the two other firms that I turned down and tell them that I was let go on my first day due to criminal charges that are now dismissed. I'm excited to see how that goes," Jaden sassed before sucking his teeth.

"Honey, don't worry about that. I already told you that Sean and I can get you into the IT department at the hospital. The only important thing is that now you have your freedom, and these charges are no longer looming over your head," Shelly reminded him as she stood up from her seat and rubbed Jaden's chin.

Jaden's smile was so big that his teeth showed before he licked his lips. Sean was so enthralled in me I caught him staring out the side of my eye. It was as if he genuinely lost interest in Shelly and barely paid attention to anything she said because the fact that he acted like he didn't just hear or see Jaden and Shelly's flirting was crazy to me.

"Shelly, please stop calling my son honey. It's a bit cringey," I confronted her, and I didn't give one fuck because Jaden was my son, and I didn't know what the fuck was going on, but I wasn't going for it at all.

"Ma, relax. Call out for the day and go and get ready because when Shelly and I get back, we're going out as a family to celebrate."

"Boy, no need to rush. All I need is ten minutes to get ready. I want to come down there with you," I explained.

Jaden shook his head dismissively. "Nah, ma. Stay here with Sean. We got this," Jaden insisted.

Sean, lost in the clouds and couldn't even see that something was going on between my son and his wife, stood up and rested both of his hands on my shoulders and kissed the side of my face. "He's right, babe. Let them go. Besides, I want you all to myself for some morning loving." Sean snickered.

"Y'all are gross, but I'll see you later, ma," Jaden said as he dragged Shelly by the wrist.

Before she left out the room, we exchanged the coldest looks. Her eyes were burning with hatred, and I could only imagine the rage in mine. The tables had turned. *I had taken her husband, and she was trying to get me back by taking my son.*

I couldn't believe things were getting messier and messier by the day. I was pregnant and in love with a man who had a wife, and my son was falling for a conniving woman who was older than me. Life couldn't have gotten any fucking weirder.

An hour later, Sean had me spawned out on the couch as he lapped up my pussy juices. My belly was so big that I couldn't even see his face from the position I was laying in. As I could do was lick my fingers as he licked my insides. I wasn't paying attention to the clock ahead of me, but he had to have been eating me for at least forty minutes. I came twice already, but he wouldn't stop. He was determined to please me, and that he did.

"Turn around, baby. I wanna hit it from the back," Sean grunted. He hopped up and grabbed a pillow and handed it to me. "Use this pillow to lean on so you're comfortable."

Sean was the most caring man I had met, and he made a complete one-eighty since finding out that I was pregnant. While I didn't like how he was treating Shelly at first, I can't say she didn't exactly deserve it. The overdose alone was enough to turn him off, and then going behind my back and keeping Jaden's arrest from me did it for me. I never wanted to take Sean away from Shelly. At first, I wasn't even down for this poly relationship in the first place, but Shelly pushed me. Shit, she even pushed Sean, and that's why we're here in the first place, but truthfully, I couldn't put all the blame on Shelly, considering that Sean and I were grown individuals and our relationship was budding. Maybe it was just in God's plan for the cards to fall how they fell.

I did as Sean directed and settled the pillow under my stomach as I tooted my ass in the air. Sean grabbed a bottle of baby oil, squirted it on my back, and began massaging me. His hands glided up and down my spine as he rubbed the oil in. He then pressed his thumbs softly into my lower back and pulsed up and down, helping to relieve the tension in my back.

"Yes, baby," I moaned. "Your hands are magic."

"Anything to make you feel like the queen you are. I just want you to remember that you're carrying a life, and this is exactly how you should be treated."

While I believed every word Sean said, seeing this much of his loving side was amazing, considering how rocky things were just a few months ago. I honestly thought that I would have been done with his ass after I went to stay by Sade's for a bit, but I'm glad I answered the phone that day because I couldn't have been happier.

"Thank you Sean, you've really been delightful," I praised him.

"You know I love you, girl. Now shut up and take this dick," he forcefully said as he slid inside me, and his dick touched my uterus.

Sean slid in and out, the gushy sounds turning me on and on as my nipples hardened. I licked my lips and played with my clit as he fucked me so good my knees, although pressed into the couch, were pulsing.

"Damn, this pregnant pussy is good, baby. It's so fucking wet. Squeeze on that dick again."

I did just as my man requested until he busted inside of my pussy and smacked my ass firmly, then massaged it quickly after.

"I'm sorry for getting carried away, but that shit is so sweet."

I licked my lips and buried my face into the couch, enjoying every inch and loving every second of lovemaking with my man.

26

LUCKY MAN

JADEN

IT FELT GOOD BEING ABLE TO HEAR THE JUDGE STATE that all charges were dismissed against me. It even felt better when Shelly kissed me.

"Congratulations, baby. I'm so happy that these charges have been dismissed, and now you can get back to your life. Before we head to the house, stop at Atmos on 125th Street. I want to pick you up something," Shelly instructed as I drove uptown.

While her gesture was cool, I wasn't in the mood to shop. I wanted to celebrate with her, Sean, and my mom, most importantly.

"Nah, baby. I want to hit Sammy's at City Island and enjoy some seafood with the family. I appreciate your gesture, but you don't have to keep buying me shit to show me your love. I'm digging you simply because of your essence. You're beautiful, smart, sexy, and sophisticated. And I enjoy the time we spend together. That's enough for me. I don't need you spoiling me like a little boy."

"But you are a little boy," Shelly retorted.

I shot her a cold look out the side of my eye as I kept my hands on the steering wheel.

"You wasn't saying that when I was balls deep in that pussy. Don't play with me, girl," I warned.

"Or what?" Shelly teased. "Lighten up, baby. I was just joking," she teased as she tickled my chin.

"Remind me you're sorry when you're sucking my dick for an hour later."

"An hour? Oh, you don't know who you're fucking with. Let me buy you a pair of sneakers, and I'll make it an hour and a half." She smirked.

"Now you're talking my language," I proclaimed as I pressed hard on the gas and shot up the Westside Highway.

It looks like we were going to Atmos after all.

Shelly wouldn't let me just cop one pair of kicks. She insisted I get three, so I did. I copped two pairs of Airforce Ones and a calm pair of New Balance. In fact, I made Shelly cop the same Airforce Ones as me so we could match. They looked so cute on her feet.

"Yeah, bae, you need those," I encouraged her.

I admired Shelly as she stood in the mirror, checking her feet out in the kicks. She was gorgeous, and her skin was flawless. I also loved her natural freckles, which she usually covered up with makeup, but today she didn't. She let me see all of her.

"I haven't worn sneakers in over fifteen years, Jaden. I don't even own a pair of sneakers."

"Exactly why you need those. If you're rolling with me, mami, you gon' have to let your hair down," I said as I snuggled behind Shelly and wrapped her into a hug. Rocking her back and forth, I kissed her on the neck, and she giggled like a little girl.

"Alright, I'll get 'em."

"That's what I thought," I said, as I smacked her ass.

Within twenty minutes, we jetted out of the spot and headed toward the parking lot.

Driving down Lenox Avenue, with the sun shining and the spring breeze beating our faces, Shelly reached over and grabbed my dick. She ran her fingers down the bulge of my print, then pulled it out. My shit instantly hardened as she lowered her head.

"Girl, what is you doing? Anybody could see us. Do you want this shit getting back to Sean?"

Shelly raised her head abruptly and eyed me suspiciously. Inching closer, she licked my ear before she whispered, "Fuck Sean."

Her words brought chills to my body, letting me know how serious she was. Damn, Shelly was cold.

"Alright then," I muttered.

Shelly poked her lips out and smirked before grabbing my junk again, and this time, when she went down, my dick hit the back of her throat. She slurped me up like an Icee. Gliding her throat up and down my shaft, she came up for air, motioned to the top, and circled the head of my dick with her tongue at least six times. That shit had me going crazy. I focused my eyes on the road ahead of me and was happy as fuck to come to a red light. As she sucked and sucked, I momentarily closed my eyes, allowing myself to enjoy the inside of her warm, gummy mouth.

Biting my lips, my body jolted as she continued to top me off.

"NAH, BOY WILDING!" I loudly heard as I opened my eyes, and the car next to me was recording us on their phone.

"Chill, bro. Hold it down!" I yelled as the car shot off ahead of me.

Honk. Honk.

"Go motherfucker!" the driver from the car behind me screamed, bringing my attention to the green light in front of me.

I pressed on the gas, still enthralled in Shelly's immaculate head game. I knew she heard that loudmouth nigga, but she refused to stop. She had my dick lock jawed in her mouth.

Damn, this was the best head I ever had.

Shelly was sucking me up so good that I had to widen my eyes just to keep them bitches open. The only head I had close to this good was a white bitch I fucked when I was in school. The bitch was a certified eater, and she'd come over just to suck my dick. We only fucked once. The pussy was mid, but that mouth was divine. Still, shit, Shelly had shorty beat.

Shelly had experience. Shelly had grace, and I can't lie. My feelings were growing stronger for her. She was a true ride-or-die. The way she looked out for my mother and the way she showed up for me when I needed her the most made me recognize that what Shelly and I had was more than just sex. We had a good time together. She was mature yet down to earth, and it felt good to be in her presence, not to mention good as hell to be in her mouth.

She hadn't come up for air yet, and my dick was so wet that I could feel the saliva drip from her mouth to my balls and between my thighs.

"Damn, Shelly," I cursed.

I thought she would ease up a bit, but my grunt caused her to go even faster and harder. Then she invited her hands into it and gave me the double twist combo and I almost thought I saw heaven.

"FUCK!" I shouted as I steadied both hands on the steering wheel.

Getting sucked up while driving wasn't easy, especially when you had a head monster like Shelly devouring your shit.

"You nasty bitch. You got me about to pull over right here. Oouuu!" I belted out as my toes twiddled and my hands jittered on the wheel.

Traffic was going so smoothly that we hadn't stopped at a red light in the last twenty minutes. I wanted to stop so badly and fuck the shit out of Shelly's mouth. She thought she was a dick-sucking pro and was trying to take advantage of me because I was driving. I couldn't let her see me sweat, so I tried my best to hold back, but she got me, and I couldn't control it.

"Fuck, I'm about to bust," I warned, waiting for her to get up so that I could wipe myself with a paper towel I had in the back seat.

Instead, Shelly kept ferociously sucking, causing me to surrender and explode in her mouth. She pressed her head further down on my dick and slurped up my nut like a vacuum. My jaw dropped at the en-joyable sensation and stayed open even after she raised up, wiped her mouth, and kissed me on the cheek. Shelly had blown my mind and knocked me out of my fucking socks.

Damn, I think I might have fallen in love with her ass just from the way she sucked my dick. Sean was a lucky fucking man.

27
DAUNTING REALITY
SHELLEY

TIME WAS GOING BY SO FAST THAT I COULDN'T BELIEVE today was Charlie's baby shower. Nude pastels of blue and pink balloons and additional decorations crowded the patio, as both Sean and Charlie wanted to be surprised by the baby's sex, so they chose not to find out the gender. Instead, they modeled the theme of the baby shower after both sexes, and they only asked for gift cards and money as gifts. That was new-age, and I had never heard of it, but it wasn't my baby or my baby shower, so I had no say so whatsoever.

Sweet sounds of nostalgic R&B played through the condo as Charlie, Sean, and I engaged the guests. Charlie was officially seven months pregnant with a high, round belly and a glow I envied. Sipping my glass of wine near the patio door, I watched our few guests. Charlie's best friend, Sade, and my and Sean's frat brothers and sorority sisters gather around Charlie, begging to rub her belly. Sean wasn't too far away either as he watched over every foot Charlie took, eyeing her with a stint of gloating concern that reminded me of how Sean once regarded me.

While I wasn't completely innocent, considering that I was fucking Jaden and actually loving it, it still cut deep to see my husband completely disregard me. Within the last three months, our sex was completely nonexistent, and Sean barely even talked to me. And although I had returned to the office and assumed my position as CNO, Sean made sure to handle all business with Charlie, who was still assisting me in my role. At home, Sean acted like he didn't even care or notice how cozy Jaden and I were becoming.

I went from having office sex with my husband and our girlfriend to sneaking in quickies at work with my girlfriend's son. Considering that Jaden was working full-time in the IT department of the hospital, we usually had lunch together, which almost always consisted of Jaden slurping the juice out of my pussy or me sucking him dry or us rolling around on the floor fighting for who would be on top during the 69.

The sex was great, and Jaden's company distracted me from the devastation I felt knowing I was losing Sean to Charlie. At least with Jaden longing after me, stimulating my mind with intellectual conversation just like Sean used to do, I didn't have to exactly wallow in misery. I could at least get the Mario coins knocked out of my pussy and be told how beautiful and smart I was, not to mention be treated on a lavish date every time Jaden got paid. Jaden gave me butterflies, and he knew how to play his part. He never grew jealous whenever Sean wanted to show his affection with an occasional disingenuous kiss or love tap. He wasn't threatening to tell Sean about us. He just played his position, and I loved that.

I was already stressing inside as Charlie grew bigger and bigger, as I knew that the elephant in the room would have to be addressed. While our condo was fabulous, it simply was not big enough for four adults and a growing baby. All three bedrooms were occupied, and it started to feel a bit stuffy when we were all in the same room. Things would soon have to change, and seeing as Sean and Charlie hadn't mentioned it, I was almost sure they were hiding their plans. It had me on edge, but I refused to pry. I instead kept myself occupied, usually with Jaden's dick in my mouth.

"Shelly, are you ready for motherhood?" One of my sorority sisters asked, startling me from daydreaming.

I turned to her and plastered a smile on my lips. "More than ever. I'm just grateful that Charlie gave up her body to give Sean and I the child we always wanted," I lied. There was no way that Sean would allow us to go public with a polyamorous affair, so we orchestrated the idea that Charlie was our surrogate.

Sean even went as far as paying a doctor off to fabricate information to support that Charlie underwent in vitro fertilization to cover our tracks. He then went to the press to score interviews ahead of the pregnancy leaking to the media. Public relations at its finest, and Sean Fox had no remorse for it. Sean said that we constantly manipulated the public to save face for the hospital, so what difference did it make if we did it for our own personal gain and to protect our image? I, of course, went along with it to save myself from public embarrassment. Although my heart was bleeding with humiliation, somehow, repeatedly telling the lie and pretending this was my baby temporarily put my heart at ease. Too bad I couldn't sleep with it.

"The things technology can do these days are amazing. I'm thrilled for you. You're going to be a great mother."

"Thank you, Soror Chaplin," I replied as I rubbed the arm of the regional director of my chapter. Chaplin was a stunning sixty-four-year-old woman, the spitting image of Vanessa Williams.

"You're welcome. If only my husband and I had this type of technology back then, we probably would have had more than two kids like we wanted, but that's water under the bridge now. It all worked out how it should have, just how it worked out for you and Sean," she responded sincerely.

I smiled again, this time showing all of my teeth.

"I'm going to get going now. My husband and I have Broadway tickets for *Wicked*. Sheryl Lee Ralph is playing the lead. We can't miss it."

"And I wouldn't want you to." I grinned before leaning forward to kiss her on both cheeks. "Thanks for coming by, Soror. Enjoy the show."

A minute after Soror Chaplin walked away, a wave of lightheadedness fanned over me. I walked back inside the house, and as soon as I turned the corner for the kitchen, vomit hurled out of my mouth. I started to feel hot as more vomit continued gushing out. As I stood up, leaning on the island, I continued to throw up all over my feet. I took one step forward, trying to reach for a paper towel, and slipped and fell right into my own vomit. All I remember was the hit being a hard thump before I blacked out.

As soon as I opened my eyes, I felt my body constricted. I attempted to raise my arms, but they were so heavy, and the right one was attached to an IV. I squinched my eyes again, settling on the nurse near the door. She walked inside with a sympathetic grin on her face.

"How are you feeling, Mrs. Fox?"

I tried to turn my neck, and my entire head started to throb. "Not so good. What happened to me? Where am I?"

"You fell and suffered from a grade three concussion, and you've been unconscious for the last three days."

My jaw fell open, which caused slight pain. I raised my hand to rub the side of my face before exhaling deeply.

"Where's my husband?"

"He hasn't been up here since the very first day. He won't return any of our calls, either."

I was thoroughly confused. Sean really didn't give a fuck about me.

"But a Jaden Thompson has been up here several times demanding to see you, but seeing as he isn't family, he has not been permitted."

My chest started to swell, and water welled up in my eyes.

"Please don't cry, Mrs. Fox. Everything will be alright. There's something else that I have to tell you that most likely contributed to your concussion."

"I'm not about to die, am I?" I asked, looking up at the nurse with pleading, serious eyes.

A smile contorted on her face. "No, not at all. Mrs. Fox, you're pregnant."

Deafness fell over my ears as I closed my eyes, unsure if I heard her right.

I haven't been pregnant in all of my adult life. This was unbelievable.

"Are you sure?"

The nurse swept her bang behind her ear and nodded three times.

"Does my husband know that I am pregnant?"

"Yes, he does. That kind of information is always disclosed to the spouse."

Holding back tears and gripping my lips together, I inhaled deeply. "Is my baby okay?"

"Yes. The fetus is still intact. And you're doing fine as well. You are required to have a full ten days of rest, which means you can be discharged as early as next week, especially if all continues to go well now that you are awake. Our main priority now is to ensure you have enough fluids and you're eating properly for the healthy growth of the baby. I need your verbal consent to take prenatal vitamins, but other than that, we are all set. Would you like to call your husband or for us to do it for you?"

I closed my eyes and opened them again, confused about what to do. There was no way Sean was the father of my child, and he knew it, which would explain why he didn't return any of the hospital's calls or even come up here to check on me. While Jaden and I have been having sex for a little over two months, I was almost certain that I conceived during the time we had sex while I was menstruating. From a young girl, I heard that having sex while on your period was the quickest way to get pregnant. And while I was fertile as fuck when I was younger, I didn't do anything additionally to add to my chances of getting pregnant, which explains why I never had sex while on my period before, despite how nasty I really thought it was.

Nonetheless, I didn't know how to feel, except that I wanted to cry. What I was most confused about was whether they were tears of joy or pain. I was finally pregnant and could have the child I always wanted, but it wouldn't be with Sean. And Sean was close to becoming a father, but I just wasn't the mother. It didn't matter how much we both lied to ourselves and each other about being content without kids. Our fate was to be parents, just not together, and we both had to accept that.

28

PRETTY WINGS

SEAN

"**S**EAN, IT'S BEEN A LITTLE OVER A WEEK SINCE we've checked in on Shelly. We need to go see her and make sure she's okay." Charlie had been buzzing in my ear for the last week about going to see Shelly.

Charlie was curious as to why I wasn't concerned about Shelly's well-being. We even got into a big argument about it, and she forced me to sleep on the couch. As much as I didn't want to argue with Charlie, I couldn't bring myself to tell her the real reason I refused to face Shelly. Too embarrassed to disclose to her that Shelly was pregnant, I bottled the feelings inside and instead drowned myself in Charlie's super wet pussy and spent the other time running several miles around Central Park and lifting heavy weights in the gym.

I know my lack of care for Shelly alarmed Charlie, but if only she knew the truth. Considering that Charlie just wouldn't let it go, I had to tell her before my nonchalance fucked up the good thing we had going. I couldn't afford to lose Charlie either, not when I was growing in love with her and our unborn baby day by day.

"Hello, do you hear me talking to you?" Charlie pestered.

I bit my bottom lip, placed my tablet on the nightstand, and removed my glasses. Seated in the bed that I'd shared with Shelly for years, I turned to face Charlie.

"I know it seems cold of me to leave Shelly in the hospital after she had a concussion, but that's not the full story."

With her eyes bulging, Charlie lowered her head and tapped her foot several times. "Look, Sean, just spit it out. We're about to have a baby. I can't take the secrets. Everything else about us has been open and fully transparent. What the fuck is going on?"

"Shelly is pregnant, and I know it's not my baby," I confessed.

Charlie's face was stony as she covered her mouth with her hands.

"I know. I was speechless too when I found out and even more speechless when security at the hospital let me know that Jaden had been up there every day to see her, but they wouldn't let him because he wasn't listed as family. The security guard told me that Jaden was saying he's the father."

The words struggled to come out like wet feet sweeping through the sand. I choked on my own fear as I lowered my eyes, refusing to look at Charlie. I held onto this information for ten damn days, and I couldn't even admit it to myself. I took a week of my vacation time just to act like I didn't know the truth. I even avoided bumping into Jaden, ensuring I was up and at the gym by five a.m., not coming back to the condo until a little after seven-thirty a.m. to ensure Jaden was gone. I made sure to monitor his movements to avoid bumping into him anywhere else in the house, and he actually made it easier by deliberately avoiding me and his mother.

Seeing as Jaden was new in his role as an IT Specialist, he worked late hours, and he visited the hospital Shelly was at every day, hoping to get through and see her. By the time he strolled into the house, I was already retired in the bedroom. I just didn't know what to say. He's a kid, and Shelly's an adult. She was to blame. There was no way I would even think about approaching Jaden, but in the same regard, I couldn't manage to look at him. All these years, Shelly rarely got her period and never got pregnant by me, yet she got pregnant by Jaden in less than six months. It truly crushed me.

"Wait. What did you just say?" Charlie was now standing beside the bed with her arms folded.

"Shelly is pregnant, and Jaden claims to be the father."

Pacing back-and-forth, Charlie fumed. "I can't say I'm surprised. There was a feeling in the pit of my stomach that something was going on between them. I tried to get you to see it many times, but you were either too enthralled in that fucking tablet or obsessed with me. Obsessed so much that you couldn't see that your wife was taking advantage of my son!" she screeched, her pitch piercing through the room.

"Keep your voice down. I'm not ready to address Jaden just yet."

"I don't give a fuck what you're ready for. I'm no longer letting this shit go on without confronting my son and Shelly's ass."

I jumped up from the bed, reaching for Charlie's arm. She yanked away and continued to hold her stance with her arms folded over her belly, a scowl plastered on her face, and her hips exaggerated to the right side. I stepped closer and closer to her as she moved back and back out of my reach.

"How long did you know?"

Continuing to step closer, I finally grabbed her by both wrists. "Look, Charlie, I've already lost Shelly. I can't lose you and my child," I wept, my voice breaking and eyes jumping as I struggled to look at her.

"HOW LONG DID YOU KNOW?" Charlie repeated, actually hollering at the top of her lungs.

"The very first day. A few hours after she was processed," I admitted.

Charlie yanked away from my hold quickly and raised her head to look me directly in the face. Eyes piercing with hatred and nostrils flaring, she rolled her shoulders back.

Smack.

In a matter of a second, Charlie had bitch slapped me so hard that I had to regain my focus.

"I'm sorry."

Slap.

Palms open and sweaty, she smacked me across the other side of my face.

"You're sorry? You left me in the dark for days, yet telling me how much you love me, and love that we can be transparent and open and how you trust me, yet you kept this from me for so long?"

With tears in my eyes, I struggled to face her. She was right.

"Charlie, I just didn't know what to say because I hadn't fully processed it yet. This is a lot for me too. Imagine how I feel? I HAVE FEELINGS TOO!" I yelled.

I was so fucked tired of having to be Batman, rescuing everyone, saving face, remaining stoic, and just accepting all the bullshit thrown my way. This time I caved. I just didn't know what to feel, say or think, let alone share that vulnerability with someone else.

Charlie exhaled deeply and wrapped me in her arms. Although she was much shorter than me with equally short arms, her hug was tight and comforting. Tears continued to flow down my face, as I wiped them back as much as I could. As Charlie hugged me tighter, I hugged her back until she motioned me toward the bed, and I sat down. Charlie sat on my lap and planted gentle pecks on my cheek as she massaged my head.

"Don't worry, baby. I'm right here, and we will get through this together as a family."

Charlie's consoling touch calmed me down, and the tears dried away. Just having her with me changed everything. I lifted my head and grabbed her lips into mine. As I kissed her softly, I rubbed her belly. Now that I released some of the pain, I was able to think clearer. I knew exactly what I had to do next, and I was happy to do it. The truth was, I was about to be a father, and now Shelly could finally experience motherhood. We just couldn't give each other the gift of parenthood but thank God we'd both be able to experience it in our lifetime. Caressing Charlie and her beautiful baby bump took all my anger away. What I was about to do would benefit us all, and I was so happy I finally came to the realization that Shelly and I just weren't meant to be.

Twenty-Four Hours Later

Shelly's face was full of shock when she saw Charlie and I stroll into her hospital room. She was sitting on the ledge, putting her shoes on, when she noticed us.

"The first thing I want to say to you is congratulations. You're going to be a mother, Shelly," I praised.

Shelly lowered her head and twiddled her thumbs, afraid to look at me.

"Look, I didn't come here to fight with you. I came here to set you free."

At the sound of those words, Shelly's face contorted in a weird grimace. Her eyes were flat and dull, and she looked out of it. "What do you mean?" she muttered.

"Shelly, I'm filing for divorce."

Shelly's brows pulled together, as she shook her head slowly. Her chest caved in as her spine curled forward. She began to rub her forehead several times before returning her gaze to me. Instantly, it became hotter in the room that was once just cool and chilly.

"Divorce? No, Sean. No," she mumbled as she stepped forward with her arms out, reaching for me.

Part of me wanted to hug her so badly, but I knew if I did, it would give off the wrong message, and the truth was I had to let her go.

"We can lie to the world all we want but we can't lie to ourselves. I know you love me, and I'll always love you, but truthfully, you'll never be happy until you're with a woman. I know it, and you know it. It's time to make yourself happy because I've found my happiness with Charlie."

Shelly's eyes shifted to Charlie as she rubbed her hands through her red bob.

"I'll be filing the paperwork tomorrow. I have no desire for this divorce to get ugly. You can have whatever you want. First, starting with the condo. It's yours. Charlie and I are moving out by the end of the week. We're going to stay at the house in Queens until we move into our own house. You and Jaden can have the condo and figure out what the next steps are for you guys," I expressed as I heard Charlie's heart thumping since she was so close to me.

Still gripping my hand tightly, Charlie stepped forward from behind my shadow so Shelly could see all of her.

"For what it's worth, Shelly, I never meant for any of this to happen. I never meant to get in the middle of you and Sean's relationship, just as much as I'm sure you never meant to seduce my son. Because you're a good woman with a heart of gold, I can overlook the fact that you took advantage of him because I know you were hurting. I just want you to know that regardless of anything, I'm still your friend and if you ever need anything, don't hesitate to ask."

Shelly's eyes were full of tears as small droplets trickled down the sides of her face like rain beating on a windowpane.

"I love you too, Shelly, and I will support you and your baby just like my own. I just refuse to deny you the happiness you truly deserve. I just pray that you don't do what you did to me, to Jaden. Don't string him along or have him think that you're all in when you're always one foot in and another foot out. Jaden's just a kid, Shelly. He doesn't deserve that. Let him go, Shelly. Let him spread his pretty wings."

Looking at Shelly was tearing me up inside. I'd never seen her this distraught. Determined to walk out of there levelheaded, I had to turn away. While I wish I could have consoled her, I knew it wouldn't change the fact that our marriage had run its course. Nothing could save us, not even Jesus himself. We just weren't meant to be, and as much as I fought it for years, and as much as it hurt to see Shelly hurt, I knew I was making the right choice for both of us. We were simply better off apart.

<h1 style="text-align:center">29</h1>

UNPREDICTABLE

SHELLY

EARING THE WORD DIVORCE FROM SEAN DEVASTAT-ed me. As much as I knew in the back of my mind where our marriage was heading, I couldn't have imagined it would happen this soon. And I would have never imagined that I'd be the one to help him find the love of his life. Never in a million years did I think Sean would fall out of love with me and into the arms of one of our girlfriends. As cliché as it was and expected by many, which explained why wives usually feared having threesomes with their husbands, I still never thought it could happen to me.

I swore I knew Sean like the back of my hand. I believed that there wasn't a woman on this earth that could take my spot. I was never intimidated by the presence of a woman because I knew no other woman could hook my husband. Seeing that I was always the one checking out women and that Sean had never cheated on me during our marriage, I was never worried about losing my man to another woman. I never thought that the fact that I was barren would really bother Sean. I thought that we both were happy without having children. I thought we were content with our full, fabulous lives so much that having biological children of our own didn't matter. If push came to shove, I was almost certain that we would just adopt. Never in a million years did I imagine I'd get pregnant by someone else, and that Sean would get another woman pregnant.

Life was truly unpredictable, just like what I was about to do. As soon as Charlie and Sean left the hospital, I took an Uber directly to Brooklyn. Luckily Sean brought me a pair of clothes, my wallet, and my phone because I was able to act on my first instinct. I took a deep breath as I was reminded where I was at. I grabbed the elaborate, heavy door gong that stood outside a beautiful brownstone on Stuyvesant Avenue in Bed Stuy. I was hoping she was home because I needed my safe space, the only person in the world that could comfort me. After knocking on the door twice, my heart began to beat harder and harder as I heard footsteps approach the other side of the door. An eyeball appeared through the peephole, and the door opened slowly.

"Shelly, what are you doing here?"

She was even more beautiful than when I last saw her at Brooklyn Museum. Dressed comfortably in a silk flowy two-piece with her spunky afro wild and free atop her head, tears filled my irises as soon as we locked eyes.

"Shyann, I love you. I don't want anyone else but you."

Shaking mildly, Shyann stepped forward and wrapped her arms around me. I lowered my head and kissed her passionately.

"I've been waiting my entire life to hear you say those words," she whispered.

Grabbing me by the hand, she led me inside.

"There's something I have to tell you. There's a lot I have to tell you, and I just hope that once I pour my heart out, you're still able to love me, as much as I love you."

Shyann motioned me over to her couch, seated in her den. The mild sun dawned on our backs and lit the entire house with a glow.

"Shelly, I want you to know that there's nothing you can ever tell me that would change how I feel about you. Nothing and I mean that!" she asserted. "What's going on, Shellz?"

"Sean and I are getting a divorce. I'm pregnant, Shyann."

To my surprise, Shyann's face perked up as she leaned forward and grabbed me into a seated hug. Rubbing my back gently, she kissed the sides of my face repeatedly.

"I'm so happy! We're having a baby, Shelly, our own baby!" she squealed.

I pulled away from her, pursuing my lips together as I searched her joy-filled eyes.

"There's something important that I must do. I have to break it off with the father. He's in love with me, and if we're going to do this the right way, I can't lead another person on that I love. I just can't."

Shyann nodded her head. "I'm proud of you, Shelly."

Two hours later, after I prepped Shyann on the entire story with Charlie and Jaden, and we laughed and cried, and she cooked for me, Jaden texted me to let me know he was outside. Things were moving so fast, and I couldn't slow it down. The truth was that I couldn't afford to wait any longer. Sean was right. I couldn't string Jaden along for the ride, knowing I didn't want him now and wouldn't want him later.

At the sound of the knock, I got up and motioned toward the door. As I peered in the peephole, I could see Jaden's budding smile through the door. I took a deep breath, preparing myself for what I was about to say. I stepped aside and opened the door. Once he saw me, his calm smile turned into a big grin.

"How are you feeling, baby?" he asked, concerned yet equally excited.

"I'm doing okay," I said in a monotone pitch as I closed the door behind him. "Follow me."

Once inside the den, where Shyann sat on a loveseat opposite of us, Jaden turned to me with a puzzled look.

"What's going on? Why am I here and who are you?" he asked all three questions shifting his glance back and forth between me and Shyann.

"Her name is Shyann, and this is her house. Please sit down, Jaden. I have to talk to you about something."

Jaden bit his bottom lip before curling it inside his mouth. He plopped down on the couch, and I followed behind him. Taking his hand into mine, I deeply exhaled as I readied myself to break his heart.

"Listen, Jaden. I just want you to know you are a force to be with. You're intelligent, articulate, fun, and funny. You have so many great things ahead of you, and I'm rooting for you every step of the way, but I asked you here to let you know I can't do this. I can't be with you."

Jaden sniffled deeply before crunching his brows and locking his jaw. "What do you mean? We're having a baby. We're starting our own family. You said you loved me, Shelly."

I glanced over at Shyann, whose eyes were damp as she eagerly watched on.

"I know, and the truth is I do love you... like a son. Jaden, what we did should have never happened, but I'm not entirely upset because you gave me something that even my husband couldn't give me, and for that reason, I will always love you, but I'm not in love with you. Truthfully, I was never in love with Sean. I have always been in love with Shyann, and now that Sean and I are getting a divorce, I can finally move on and be happy with the woman I've been in love with since I was nineteen years old."

Jaden sniffled again as a lone tear trickled down the side of his face. "So, you're telling me that what we had meant nothing to you? I MEANT NOTHING TO YOU!" he screamed as he pulled away from me.

"No, no, not at all. You mean a lot to me. You mean so much to me that I have to let you go. I can't hurt another person who I love. It's not fair to you, and I can't live with myself knowing I hurt someone who loves me simply because I can't love them back the way they need to be loved."

Jaden wiped his eyes and lifted his chin as he nodded rapidly. "And what about my child? Our child?"

"You'll always be the father, and I'll never keep the baby away from you, but there is no future for you and me. I'm sorry, Jaden."

Jaden got up from the couch and walked toward the exit. "You know, I really thought that what we had was special. I thought that as soon as Sean found out you were pregnant, he'd divorce you, and we'd start our family. I can't believe I lost my mother, and I lost you. After it's all said and done, I'm the one out here alone."

Rushing to Jaden's side, I held him in my arms. His sobs became louder and louder. "You're not alone, Jaden. You're not alone."

As I rocked him back and forth, I felt a touch on my shoulder. I turned my head slightly right, and there was Shyann, standing there with a messy face of tears. She stepped forward and wrapped her arms around both of us.

"Neither one of you is alone. As long as there is breath in my lungs, both of you and our unborn child will never be without," Shyann vowed as she rubbed both of our backs.

EPILOGUE
CHARLIE FOX

Three Years Later

"*SEANY, COME ON. YOU'RE GOING TO MAKE US LATE* for Auntie Shelly's wedding!" I exaggerated as I chased my hyperactive toddler around the foyer of our massive New England estate.

Jaden, his fiancée, and my granddaughter, Jayda, were already loaded up in the Suburban waiting on us so we could all drive across the lake to Shelly and Shyann's cottage for their ceremony. Situated on fifty-one acres in Darien, Connecticut, the Fox Estate was comprised of three mansions. Sean and I shared one, Shelly and Shyann had one, and Jaden, the last mansion belonged to Jaden and his fiancée. The six of us operated as a family, under a one hundred billion dollar bond and trust, never having to pay taxes or bills ever again. Yet, we still generated our own revenue, having ten subdivision buildings, five of which would soon be turned into profitable businesses. We currently only have one up and running, Fox Luxury Suites & Homes, our family-owned premier hotel, with immediate plans to start a hospital in the next five years.

"No, mommy! No!" Desean Jr. bickered, throwing a slight temper tantrum.

Sick of his shit, I took a careful step forward, ensuring I didn't slip on our marble tiles, and yanked him off the floor. He started to squabble a bit until I poked him under his underarms and began tickling him. He laughed aloud, cooing and fidgeting in my arms.

"See, mommy knows your spot. She sure does." I chuckled as I tickled him over and over.

Now that I had my baby bag on my shoulder and Seany in my arms, I grabbed the door and stepped outside. Luckily, Sean was right there to help, like always. He truly was a wonderful dad and an even better husband. It'd been two and a half years since I gave birth. And immediately after the paternity test determined Sean was indeed Seany's father, Sean proposed. We waited a year, giving Shelly enough time to give birth before we got married, as we were her and Shyann's support system throughout Shelly's entire pregnancy. I couldn't be happier to finally be a wife, a new mother, and even a grandmother. Life had indeed turned around for me, and I couldn't be more thankful. In fact, life was treating us all well, and I was happy to have an entire support system that all shared the same last name as me.

"Go to daddy!" I shooed as I forced Seany into his father's hands.

Dressed in a classic black tux, Sean never looked better. At the age of forty-four, Sean was aging like fine wine, just getting better with time. He'd since grown out a scruffy, well-groomed beard that gave him an edgy sex appeal, especially for a light-skinned dude. It felt good to look at my man and know I didn't have to share him.

"You look beautiful, baby," Sean complimented me as he leaned in for a kiss. I returned the pressure, pulling on his bottom lip, as we squished Seany between us, smothering each other with love.

Once we broke the embrace, I smiled, genuinely ecstatic because Sean just had a way of always making me feel special, truly like the only girl in the world.

"Thanks, baby. You're looking good too."

Sean lowered his head, avoiding my eye contact.

"You okay?"

He took a deep breath and exhaled deeply. "Yeah. I just can't believe Shelly is really marrying a woman. I mean, I'm happy for her. It's just so surreal."

As I slammed the door shut, picked up the end of my bridesmaid gown, and began walking, Sean followed me. "I know, baby. It's crazy, but I'm so glad Shelly has finally made herself happy."

"So am I. I just never really imagined it. Time, therapy, and having you by my side every step of the way has truly helped me to make peace with all of this."

"We've come a long way, baby, and I'm happy for all of us, especially Jaden. I thought he'd never get over Shelly, so I am delighted he found Melody."

"Yeah, me too. I'm mature, but I ain't that mature to watch a knucklehead who I treat like a son with my ex-wife." Sean chuckled as he leaned down to place Seany in his car seat.

"What so funny?" Jaden asked from inside the car.

"Oh, nothing," I replied as I waited for the driver to open the passenger seat.

"Good afternoon, Mrs. Fox," our Middle Eastern driver said, greeting me.

"Good afternoon, thank you," I responded.

As soon as Sean and I got into the car, the driver locked the doors and rolled down the driveway of my and Sean's house. The cottage home was only a five-minute drive, yet there was so much greenery and beautiful scenery to see on the way. The fact that it was all ours was the best part. We had been owners of this estate for the last eleven months, and it still blew my mind.

Looking out the window in awe, I blinked twice as we approached the cottage where the wedding was held. From the outside, there were white horses along the garden full of roses and daises situated around the Grecian water fountain. When Shelly said she wanted to get married on our property, at the cottage home, I couldn't imagine her vision. Yet, as we pulled into the parking lot-sized driveway, her vision was clear.

The driver opened our doors, and we stepped out of the car, looking regal and sophisticated. Jaden had sniped his locs last year and was sporting a light Caesar cut, which gave him a cleaner look. Jaden's fiancée' Melody had glazed chocolate skin and micro locs that looked so delicious on her. Although she had locs, she knew how to dress them up and always look classy, and that was just one thing I liked about her, amongst many. The fact that she was at the top of her game in her respective field of hospitality at the age of twenty-six years old, having run several Disney properties across the world, was another thing I liked about her. In fact, she was the reason behind us opening Fox Luxury Suites & Homes, and she served as the managing director while Sean serves as the CEO and Jaden spearheads all the IT.

"Ma, do you need me to watch Seany?" Melody asked as we walked up the driveway.

"Thanks for asking, baby girl, but don't worry about it. You two got your hands full with Jayda," I responded, alleviating them from my terrible two toddler, who were much more of a handful than my granddaughter.

"No problem, ma," Jayda replied.

Thirty minutes later, we all took our seats in the breathtaking garden amongst Shelly's sorority sisters, our Presbyterian colleagues, and other relatives. Chrisette Michele's "You Mean That Much To Me" dawned over us at a moderate volume, filling our hearts with emotion. Out walked Shelly and Shyann, both wearing gorgeous lace gowns. Shelly's gown was mermaid constructed, while Shyann's was in an A-line off-the-shoulder sleeveless design. Hand in hand, they walked down the aisle together. Their makeup was flawless, and both of their natural hair was styled in updos. Shelly sported her natural red hair, while Shyann also rocked her natural kinky coils.

They slowly made it to the altar, where the queer, female-presenting officiator stood with a bright smile before Chrisette Michele's voice waned and the music cut off.

"Hello, everyone. We are here to celebrate and commemorate the union of Mrs. and Mrs. Shenelle Fox. Many of you may be wondering why a lesbian would want to take the last name of her wife's ex-husband. Well, let me just say if it were me, I'd do the same thing. Have you googled Sean Fox?" the officiator jested, and we all busted out laughing.

"I kid. I kid. Both of our lovely brides are just as accomplished and loaded themselves. And today, they will come together as one. Now which one of you lesbos is going first? It's equal opportunity all up and through here."

"She's hilarious," I whispered into Sean's ear as the rest of the audience chuckled.

He nodded his head in agreement and squeezed my hand.

Shyann lifted her hand.

"The lady in white shall go first. Oh shit, they're both in white," the officiator joked again.

Shyann pulled out her phone and scrolled through it. "I didn't want to write out any corny vows because, truly, I've already put in my for better or worse dues. Shelly and I know how we both rock and have decided to keep our exact vows personal. Nonetheless, I would like to read a scripture from the Holy Bible that describes exactly how I feel about you, Shelly. Few people understand how majestically racy the book Songs of Solomon is, but as I was reading it one night, it blew my mind. Let's go to the Songs of Solomon, book 4. And it goes like this:

You are beautiful, my darling,

beautiful beyond words.

Your eyes are like doves

behind your veil.

Your hair falls in waves

like a flock of goats winding down the slopes of Gilead.

Your teeth are as white as sheep,

recently shorn and freshly washed.

Your smile is flawless,

each tooth matched with its twin.[a]

Your lips are like scarlet ribbon.

your mouth is inviting.

Your cheeks are like rosy pomegranates

behind your veil.

Your neck is as beautiful as the tower of David,

jeweled with the shields of a thousand heroes.

Your breasts are like two fawns,

twin fawns of a gazelle grazing among the lilies.

Before the dawn breezes blow

and the night shadows flee,

I will hurry to the mountain of myrrh

and to the hill of frankincense.

You are altogether beautiful, my darling,

beautiful in every way.

Come with me from Lebanon, my bride,

come with me from Lebanon.

Come down from Mount Amana,

from the peaks of Senir and Hermon,

where the lions have their dens

and leopards live among the hills.

[9]You have captured my heart,

my treasure my bride.

You hold it hostage with one glance of your eyes,

with a single jewel of your necklace.

[10] Your love delights me,

my treasure, my bride.

Your love is better than wine,

your perfume more fragrant than spices.

[11]Your lips are as sweet as nectar, my bride.

Honey and milk are under your tongue.

Your clothes are scented

like the cedars of Lebanon.

You are my private garden, my treasure, my bride,

a secluded spring, a hidden fountain.

Your thighs shelter a paradise of pomegranates

with rare spices—

henna with nard,

nard and saffron,

fragrant calamus and cinnamon,

with all the trees of frankincense, myrrh, and aloes,

and every other lovely spice.

You are a garden fountain,

a well of fresh water

streaming down from Lebanon's mountains."

As Shyann finished her monologue, Shelly's eyes were dripping with water. Shelly grabbed Shyann's hands into hers and stepped directly in front of Shyann's face.

Holding back tears, Shelly's groggy voice dawned on us. "Baby. It's been a long time coming, and I just want to thank you for being patient with me. I have never loved anyone as much as I've loved you, that is until I gave birth to our beautiful daughter Jayda. You mean so much to me, and I am so happy that we get to spend the rest of our life together..."

THE END

ABOUT THE AUTHOR

Penny Blacwrite is the #1 bestselling author of *Charlie's Angels: A Polyamorous Affair* and the award-winning poetry book *For Every Black Woman's Soul.* Also, she is a published journalist with credits in *Amsterdam News, Our Times Press*, and online entertainment publications *Parle Magazine* and *Enstarz*. Groomed as a student reporter from the age of twelve, Penny was trained by some of the best leading industry writers and journalists from *News Day, 60 Minutes*, CBS, and NBC. Since then, Penny had a knack for storytelling.

As a novelist, Penny writes twisted, forbidden romances, women's fiction and erotica. Nonetheless, she has always longed to tell stories that mirrored her experiences in authentic, creative ways. From being born in prison and raised as a Tupac baby to attending the illustrious Howard University, Penny's real life is the launching pad for her intricate plots, mind-blowing secrets and explosive endings.

Penny is a New Yorker residing in Atlanta with her MacBook, and a mind full of chatter that makes for great stories. Lastly, she is currently studying for her MFA in Creative Writing where she has dreams of launching a specialized niche course focused on self-publishing and rapid releasing at an accredited university.

MAILING LIST

Subscribe to my mailing list for updates, cover reveals and prizes.

GLOSSARY

Dear Readers,

This book is set in New York City between several boroughs, primarily Manhattan and Brooklyn. As a native New Yorker from Bedford Stuyvesant, also known as Bed Stuy, Brooklyn, I thought it only fitting to provide a glossary of New York and other general lingo to better understand and enjoy the story. See below:

1. Prophyte: an older member of an NPHC or cultural-based organization.

Ex: I needed that nurturing from a prophyte, from a woman I admired and a woman who I was once deeply in love with. (Chapter One)

2. NYCHA: New York City Housing Authority (better known as the agency that owns the projects.

Ex: I took a deep breath, inhaling the stale smell of NYCHA (New York City Housing Authority), better known as the projects, and knocked on Sade's door. (Chapter Two)

3. Preeing: Watching, studying, analyzing.

Ex: "Nigga, don't watch me. Watch TV. Why the fuck you preeing the next man's face for, anyway?" I threw back, challenging him. (Chapter Eight)

4. Cut Yo' Ass: Roast you.

Ex: "Don't make me cut yo' ass." (Chapter Eight)

5. Pack You Up: Roast you to the highest level, then finish you and send you off.

Ex: "Don't make me cut yo' ass and pack you the fuck up." (Chapter Eight)

6. Son: a term of endearment, unisex, can be used on men and women.

Ex: C'mon, son. Look at you. (Chapter Eight)

7. Whip: car.

Ex: "You ain't got no whip." (Chapter Eight)

8. Breesh: bread, money.

Ex: "You ain't got no whip, no bitch, and no breesh." (Chapter Eight)

9. Fly: fire, fresh, of good taste.

Ex "Ma, that shit is fly." (Chapter Fifteen)

10. Bugging: out of your mind.

Ex: "You're bugging."

11. Chiefing: guarding the blunt like a chief. Holding or smoking the blunt for too long when you should puff, puff, pass.

12. Tight: upset, angry, frustrated, or irritated.

Ex: While I was tight that I couldn't stay at Sean and Shelly's condo, nothing beats having a place to call my own. (Chapter Nineteen)

13. Bread: money.

Ex: The bread I dropped on that dinner at Ruth Chris was nothing compared to what my mom has done for me. (Chapter Nineteen)

14. Buck50: a cut across the face so deep it left a nasty scar.

Ex: I gave a few niggas a Buck50, but I never killed a nigga with no blade. (Chapter Nineteen)

PENNY'S READER COMMUNITY

Thank you so much for your continued support! Follow me on the

following platforms:

Facebook Group: 5 ★ Page Turners by Penny Blacwrite

Instagram: @pennyblacwrites

Tumblr Blog: For Every Black Woman's Soul
Thank you again.
~Penny Blacwrite